Is There Not A Cause

R.E.ANTCZAK

CHAPTER ONE

One of the most important nights of his life and Drew Richards was stuck in a self checkout line at the Savemart Supercenter. His phone vibrated. He checked the text. It was Jen.

Where are you?

He thumbed a reply-

Sorry. Last minute traffic stop. An hour of paper work. Be there soon.

Jen messaged again-

Hurry! Were supposed to be at my parents in twenty minutes.

Drew lost the cell back in his jacket. Rather than decipher the signature tattooed on the woman's

3

neck in front of him, he inspected the bouquet of roses in his hand. Several petals showed signs of wilting. Savemart's best. Not exactly what he'd planned but by the time he'd made it out of the precinct the floral shop had already closed. It'd be alright, though. Jen's attention wouldn't be on the flowers, anyway.

He fished a velvet box from his khaki's, opened it. Two carats. Defiantly not a Savemart's best, but certainly his. The ring was well above what he could comfortably afford. But, only for the time being. One more year and he'd be through with law school, trade in his badge for a local firm, giving his pay scale the boost it needed to be worthy of the ring and of Jen. That's what he'd told himself when he made the purchase a couple months back and what he'd told Jen's father a few days after, when he'd asked for his daughters hand in marriage. Tonight, after dinner, on bended knee with Jen's parents looking on, he planned to do just that. That is, if he ever got there. The line still hadn't moved.

At the front of the store, a middle aged couple entered dusting snow from their jackets. Drew frowned. The streets were already slick. Traffic was going to get brutal.

What else could possibly go wrong?

The woman ahead of him darted toward an open register. Drew secured the ring in his pocket, stepped up for the next available.

A little girl, all bright eyes and pigtails, shot out of the arcade, wriggled around an oncoming cart, and raced down the front walkway to the women's restroom. Drew might have been indifferent to the incident, thought it just a fleeting observation, but something peculiar caught his eye. A woman thumbing through pamphlets at the photo shop next to the arcade had glanced after the girl. It was a subtle gesture. Drew doubted if anyone else had caught it. Certainly not the older boy still in the arcade dancing with a joystick and saving the world from alien invaders. Even if he had, it was a mere glance, seemingly innocent. But still, it was odd how the woman had noticed the girl with her back turned and her attention on the display. Also odd, was the fact that the woman had been in front of the photo shop since he'd gotten in line, and she hadn't pulled a single pamphlet. Her hands were empty...and large. Her shoulders were broad, freakishly so. And, below her coat, her calves were thick and masculine.

"Hey buddy, you're up," someone said.

At the register, Drew scanned the roses, fed his card into the machine, and chanced a look over his shoulder. The woman was gone. He didn't bother with the receipt, just hurried to the front of store.

Through the exit doors, heavy snowfall blanketed the outside. To his left, the woman who'd stood at the photo shop, with the big hands and

5

masculine calves, was nearing the restroom.

Drew glanced at the roses, then at the exit, and then back at the woman.

Don't do it...

But she did. She followed after the girl into the restroom. Only, she wasn't a she. The woman was a man. Drew was certain of it.

This can't be happening. Not now!

A store manager appeared from a darkened checkout lane, hurried past the restrooms. Her hair was short, butch. She growled into a walkie-talkie. Drew heaved a sigh of resolve, turned away from the exit doors, the snowfall, dinner with Jen and her parents, and his marriage proposal, and bee lined towards her.

"Excuse me, uh..." he read the tag on her vest, "...Alex."

The woman silenced her assault into the handheld, snapped, "Can I help you?"

"There's a little girl in the bathroom, dark hair, brown coat. Could you check on her, make sure she's ok."

"Why wouldn't she be?"

The restroom door was silent. Drew said, "I

just watched a man go in there."

"A man?"

"Yes, a man. He has on woman's clothes and a wig. But, he's definitely a man. I saw him go in after the girl."

"Okay, well, it is possible the person you saw might be a transgender? He does have a right to be in there."

Thorns dug into Drew's palm. He said, "Look, I'm a cop, off duty, I know the law. All I'm asking you to do is check on the girl. See if she's o.k."

"Sure," Alex crossed her arms. "But again, why wouldn't she be?"

Drew headed for the restroom.

"Hey, you're not allowed in there!" Alex called for security.

Drew went in anyway. The bathroom appeared empty. The only sound was the drone from the lights. To Drew's right was a three-sink vanity. Butted against it, a row of stalls. They lined the same wall and created an aisle with the opposite. Drew crossed the room, knocked over a wet floor sign. The hard plastic slapped on the tile. The man, hunched at the farthest door, reeled. His wig was disheveled and hung off center. His whole appearance seemed absurdly

7

bizarre, comical. But, there was nothing funny about his intentions, clearly evident by his twisted expression.

He charged, tried to barrel past. Drew snatched him up by the coat, slammed him against the wall. The guy let out a grunt but it didn't slow his efforts to try and escape. He struggled to pull away, took a swing. Drew evaded the blow, landed one of his own-a quick jab to the mouth- just as the bathroom door burst open. The man sank to the ground. Alex rushed in, knelt to aid him.

The man stammered, "I...I was just going to bathroom. He attacked me!"

Alex glared up at Drew, "What's wrong with you!"

Several others had entered behind her, a security guard, and a couple kids holding cell phones recording the scene. A woman, frantic and worried looking, shouldered past Drew and scooped up the little girl who'd come out of the stall.

The rose bouquet that Drew had bought for Jen lay scattered and trampled. Everyone stared at him. Not like he'd just saved a little girl from some sick pervert, but like he was the monster.

CHAPTER TWO

Drew hadn't had contact with anyone from the outside in over two years, hadn't expected, nor wanted anyone to be waiting for him when he walked out of Minnesota's State Penitentiary into the crisp, autumn morning sunlight. But, Marcus Sanchez was there. He was at the curb leaning against the grill of a blue Pacifica minivan.

Drew shook his head, said aloud, "Should have known."

Marcus, twenty-nine, a year older than Drew, grinned perfect white teeth. They contrasted well with his jet black hair and sandy complexion.

He said, "Hey, still partners right?"

Drew didn't answer, just smiled, didn't put

much into it. He and Marcus may have been friends, best friends even, but they hadn't been partners since Manslow had filed charges and Drew had been suspended. And, when the judge found Drew guilty of aggravated assault with motivated bias, he'd been stripped of his badge completely, sentenced to three years. Changing the subject, he nodded at the van, said, "Where's the Impala?"

"Traded her in. Me and Deena, we got hitched."

"Saw the ring, figured as much. When?"

Marcus glanced at his hand, said, "Early March." His smile faded "I wanted you as my best man, if you'd been out. You know that, right?"

Drew shoved his hands in his jacket, toed a piece of gravel. "It's fine, really. I'm happy for you two."

Marcus said, "Deena's pregnant, bro."

Drew didn't look up. He said, "That's great. That's what she wanted, right. To be a mom. When'd you find out?"

"Bout six months ago."

"Congratulations."

From far off a bird shrilled.

Marcus said, "Sorry about Jen, I didn't think she'd bail on you like that."

Miles of trees and grassland, colored from the cold, seemed to stretch farther from outside the prison yard. Drew let his attention drift higher searching for the distant caller. He said, "It's alright. She deserves better than a convict."

"Come on, ese, you know it's not like that. Manslow got it on three separate counts. If you wouldn't have intervened when you did, he would have done the same to that girl. You're a hero, bro."

Hero...

Drew scoffed, kept his eyes locked on the hard blue horizon. His words came out calm but sounded as far away as the view. He said, "I'm taking it the world's not looking for a hero. They could have revoked my sentence, after Manslow's arrest. It was obvious he'd lied about me attacking him. But they didn't."

"I know, man. That wasn't right." Marcus scuffed the ground with his boot. He said, "That why you stopped taking visitors, wouldn't accept my calls?"

Drew didn't reply, although, that was exactly why. The community he'd given five years to serve and protect had turned their back on him. The media had dragged his name through dirt, made him out to be some crazed anti LGBTQ terrorist and the legal system had washed their hands of him, locked him away with murderers, rapists, and thieves. Some of which he'd arrested himself, had testified against, and had helped in getting them prison time. Some of them remembered. It had been a rough three years. He said, "I did what I had to."

Marcus scoffed, said,. "Yeah, I guess."

He sounded hurt. For that, Drew was sorry. Marcus had stuck by him the whole time, had done what he could, was there now. It wasn't his fault. But, he'd asked and Drew had told him the truth.

They both were silent.

Marcus said, "Well, at least tell me you finished your law degree." His tone was lighter, easy, forgiving.

Drew felt relieved, grinned, said, "Had to do something to keep me occupied."

"Well alright then," Marcus slapped Drew on the shoulder, "hop in ese and lets go celebrate. And don't worry about nothing. You can stay with me and Deena till you pass the bar, get a job on a firm just like you wanted. It'll be like old times. Me and you kickin' tail and takin' names."

He started to turn, Drew didn't move.

"I can't go back."

"What are you talking about?" Marcus tone was no longer light or easy.

"Look Marcus, we've been friends a long time. I just..." Drew hesitated, knew his words would wound, again. Another reason why he'd ended communication, why he hadn't wanted anyone there when he got out. He didn't want to have to explain himself, knew no one would understand. How could they? They hadn't walked in his shoes, hadn't had their life taken and torn apart. He steeled himself, said, "There's nothing in Wakefield to go back to."

Marcus flinched. His mouth dropped in apparent disbelief. He said, "That's loco, bro. You got your family, the department. They've been on your side since day one. And you got a whole church full of people who love you, man. Been praying for you every week. You're not alone, bro."

Drew sighed, dug his hands deeper into his pockets, said, "I know, and I'm grateful. But that's not what I mean."

"So what do you mean?"

"I know you want me to come back, pick up where I left off, just move forward...but I can't. I don't know what forward looks like. I mean, you and Deena, married, kid on the way. Your life has moved on. I'd still

13

be living in the past."

Marcus looked puzzled.

Drew said, "I don't know how else to explain it. I just need time to figure things out. I can't do that in Wakefield, ya know."

Marcus stared hard for a moment, said "No, not really," And then his expression softened. He said, "But, then again, you always were the philosophical one. I never understand half the mess that goes on in that head of yours."

Drew laughed, accepting his friend's apparent forgiveness, again.

Marcus asked, "So, Confucius, what's the plan?"

Drew pulled a bus ticket from his jacket, held it up. "Compliments of the State. Also gave me two hundred bucks. Gate money. Figured I'd see where it leads."

Marcus frowned. "That's it? That's the plan? For such a big thinker, that's the best you came up with?"

"It's a start."

"Yeah, that's about it."

"That's all I have."

The shrill came again, more faint, farther off.

"Well, let me at least give you a ride to the bus station."

Drew smiled, didn't put much into it.

"What?"

"I think I want to walk for awhile."

Marcus combed his fingers through his hair, "Come on ese, the next towns over twenty miles. Let me give you a ride."

"I've been locked up a long time, really I just wanna walk, think for a bit."

Marcus sighed, said, "Alright, if that's what you want. But before you go, I got something for you. Well, Deena got it for you."

He got into the van, came back, said, "Deena thought you might need this."

He held out a Bible. It was new, bound in soft leather, similar to the one Drew had brought into prison, had read daily, like he was accustomed to doing, being that he'd grown up in church and had been led to the Lord at the age of seven. But, after awhile, his devotions were less frequent. And, after Manslow's trial, he'd stopped reading and praying altogether. Eventually, his Bible had become lost, or stolen, forgotten.

Drew accepted the gift. The weightiness of God's word felt good in his hand, familiar. He slipped his bus ticket inside the cover, tucked the Bible in his jacket.

"You're a blessed man, Marcus. Deena's a good woman. Tell her thanks, and that I love her. You too, man."

"Yeah, same ese. Stay in touch. And, if you ever need anything, you call me. We'll be praying for you."

They shook hands. Marcus pulled Drew in, hugged him. And then he got in the van and drove off. Drew watched after him until his friend was no longer visible. Then he turned, faced the long stretch of empty road and started walking.

CHAPTER THREE

"We have seven…"

There was a cold, hard, silence on the other end of the cell and then a voice spoke. It was calm, colder, and much harder than the silence.

"Miss Charvis, this is not the first time there have been complications with your…procedures… to come through with product. You are aware of the concept of supply and demand. If I cannot meet my customer's demand then my customer will seek another supplier who can, and I will no longer have a customer. I've provided you a very lucrative salary to make sure that doesn't happen. So do your job. The order is for ten, clean, full term, specimens each month-non negotiable. If you can't handle that then I will get someone else who can."

"That won't be necessary."

Silence. And then, "Good. My technician will meet you at the designated location at the end of month as scheduled. Is there anything else, Miss Charvis?"

"No."

"Very well...And Miss Charvis, know that I find complications very...complicated. And, I don't do complicated. I like things to be neat and clean. And if it's not, I sever the complication. Am I clear?"

"Yes."

"Good night, Miss Charvis."

The call went dead.

CHAPTER FOUR

Drew's tee was soaked. His hair hung in his eyes and beads of sweat ran into his beard. He didn't mind. He liked this kind of work; hard labor under a hot sun. It kept his physique tight and his skin tough like leather. It was the kind of work that didn't ask questions, paid in cash and usually only lasted a couple weeks which was about as long as he could stay in one place before he'd get the itch to move on. And, it was the only kind of work Drew had known since he'd left prison roughly two years ago.

He pried a damaged stud from a skid, tossed the salvageable portion on the pile to be repaired. When he did, he spotted Gus, the guy who'd hired him, step out of an office shack across the supply yard and make his way over. Gus swung a clip board and drug a handkerchief across his brow.

"How ya doing, Richards? Sure is a scorcher out here, isn't it?"

Drew said, "Spent some time down south, days were hotter, different kind of heat though, not as humid."

Gus glanced at the mounds of torn down skids behind Drew. His mouth frowned in apparent approval. He said "I guess you have. You did all this since this morning?"

Drew nodded.

"Listen," Gus shoved the handkerchief in his jeans, "I don't know what your employment situation is, what it is you're looking for, but, why don't you come work for me full time. I can really use a guy with your, eh, work ethic. I mean, I know you've only been with us a couple weeks but, man alive Richards, you do more work in a day than most of those yahoos from the temp agency do all week. I'll pay you a salary, set you up as leadman. Not here, of course, shop across town. Shutting this place down, selling it. Isn't worth the upkeep. That's why I took you on. Help get this place cleaned up, salvage what we can. But, there's not much more to do-a day or two at the most. And, I'm afraid I can't have you at the other shop, not unless you're on the payroll, you know, insurance reasons-that sort of thing. But, you'd have health benefits, 401k. It's a good opportunity and I think it'd benefit us both."

The supply yard was all dirt and weeds, and bare of any supply. Past the chain-link, field and trees covered the slope, and ran into what looked like an abandoned rail yard. It also was surrounded by rusted barb and chain-link.

Drew said, "I appreciate the offer, I really do, but, I'm just passing through."

Gus smirked, "Yeah, I figured it was something like that."

A bird circled above the train yard.

Gus said, "You know, Rocktown used to be the industrial capital of the mid-west. That station down there, they used to be so busy, I mean, hauling freight at all hours of the day and night. With all the banging and grinding, you could hardly hear yourself think. I used to get so stinking mad if I didn't make it across Fulton and Kishwaukee by five ten. Getting stuck at those tracks watching cargo for twenty minutes. And, they were precise, too. Five ten on the dot. You could set your watch by it."

Drew tried to envision the rail yard the way Gus described it. It was a hard sell. The tracks were buried underneath weeds and grass. Its buildings were nothing more than large heaps of rotted wood. If it weren't for a couple box cars, spaced out on the property, he wouldn't have been able to tell what the land had been used for.

Gus said, "Now it's a waste of space and an eye sore. Sort of like this place. Guess you got to know when to cut your losses, let go, and move on."

Drew couldn't have agreed more.

"Anyway," Gus said, "the reason I came out here was to let you know there's several dozen sacks of cement out front. Why don't you wrap this up and go help Alonzo load em' on the truck. After that, go ahead and call it a day. Margie'll have your pay in the front office. Be back Monday morning, see if we can't get things finished up out here."

"Sure thing," Drew said.

Gus started to turn, added, "And Richards, if you change your mind, about my offer, you let me know."

It was nearly 5:00 pm when Drew collected his pay from Margie and began his trek to his apartment. The sun was still up, wouldn't be dark for several hours. The temperature had cooled.

Ten minutes later, he neared Fulton and Kishwaukee. There was no traffic and the railroad tracks were deathly silent. He crossed without waiting.

Another fifteen minutes and he was out of the industrial neighborhood, heading down Huron, towards Ninth. From there, his apartment was due west just shy of a mile.

Two blocks short of Ninth, protesters rallied. From their signs, they were from New Creation Baptist Church. They stood in front of a stone building that might have been an early century school house or town hall. The images on their signs left no speculation as to what the place was used for now-an abortion clinic.

Drew wasn't opposed to the protest. He held to the same biblical view of life at conception, thought abortion to be nothing short of murder.

From across the street, a couple of the protesters stared. Not so much in a suspicious manner, like they had every other night this week. Now, they seemed curious. Drew gave a nod. One protester waved.

A string of cars cruised by. The drivers kept their gaze fixed ahead, presumably, because they didn't want to be bothered with the horrors that were being allowed to take place in their city. Or, perhaps, they just didn't care. Drew thought it might be both.

When he neared the end of the building, he spotted a woman; mid twenties, long caramel colored hair. He recognized her, watched her hand a younger woman some literature. Her manner appeared gentle and kind. Very different from her stand-off against a couple of officers who tried break up the rally Tuesday night. Her knowledge of the first amendment and her courage to stand up for her rights , even against threats of being hauled off to jail if she didn't shut her mouth, had been impressive. And apparently, effective. There she was, free from jail and still exercising her constitutional liberties. For some reason, Drew found himself smiling.

A car sped past. The driver hollered, "Why don't you just leave them alone, let them make their own choices, you judgmental....," the crudeness was lost to distance.

The younger woman, the one who'd received the literature, suddenly turned, hurried toward the parking lot. The caramel haired woman looked after her. Drew was certain there were tears in her eyes. His smile vanished.

And then, the abortion clinic, the protesters, and the woman with the caramel colored hair, were behind him. Twenty more minutes and he was rounding the wood stained stairwell of Harvey Manor, up to the third floor, where he let himself into his apartment. It wasn't much; shoddy, and in desperate need of a face lift, just like everything else in the neighborhood. But, it met his needs; semi-furnished, all utilities paid, even came with a twenty four inch color television that was useful for catching the news. Most importantly, it was week to week, no lease.

Drew showered, opted not to shave, again. He threw on a pair of sweatpants, left his upper half bare since there was no central air in the building. Fortunately, a soft breeze was coming in through the living room window. He microwaved some left over macaroni, noted he was due for stop at the corner mart and, after eating and cleaning up, he stretched out on the sofa. The imitation leather felt cool on his back, and within a few minutes he dozed off.

When he awoke, it was dark. Stretching, he grabbed the remote, clicked on the ten o'clock news, caught the tail end of an interview with an animal rights activist who ranted that his organization wasn't going to stop until every last guinea pig was free from the horrors of a laboratory cage. The news reporter ended the story by stating the group would be holding a rally in front of some location that Drew wasn't familiar with, and that all of them there at the station wished the protesters the best.

A gun went off, or maybe a car backfired, both were frequent in the area. It sounded blocks away but Drew still went to the window, looked out. Other than the lampposts humming, the neighborhood was silent, indifferent. Drew shut the window and went to bed

CHAPTER FIVE

Saturday afternoon was a refreshing seventy five degrees, clear blue sky, perfect weather for a stroll along the riverfront, which was the only semblance of beauty Drew had found in Rocktown. When he reached Levins Park, he spotted a bench, pulled out a bottled water and the Bible Marcus had given him from the duffle draped over his shoulder. Accepting the shade from a large oak, he sat back and began to read.

He'd gone through a couple chapters, when someone said, "Hi there."

He looked up. A woman approached holding several stuffed lunch bags in one arm, and in the other, a handful of gospel tracts. He knew what they were, because he'd given them out with his church, back in Minnesota. He also knew who the woman was, because he'd seen her before. She was one of the protesters from the abortion clinic, the one with the caramel colored hair.

The woman said, "I didn't mean to bother you, just thought you might be interested in some lunch." She stood a few feet away, had on scrubs, like a nurse. Her eyes were bright, almond shaped and brown. Several other church members, some Drew recognized from the clinic, were scattered throughout the park, proselytizing anyone who slowed down long enough to listen.

Drew said, "Oh, no, I'm not homele...," he recognized the irony before he finished. He may have had a roof over his head, but, it definitely wasn't a home. He said, "I mean, I'm good, but thanks."Again, irony. He wasn't good.

"Oh, okay." The woman gestured, said, "Is that a Bible?"

Drew said it was.

"So, are you a Christian?"

Drew let his eyes fall. No one had asked him that in a long time. It had been just as long since he'd initiated the fact. When he lifted his gaze, the woman was smiling. Her eyes were aglow with what he took to be joy. It was comforting.

"I am," He said, although, he didn't put much into it. He said, "My grandfather's a Baptist preacher. I grew up in his church. He led me to the Lord when I was seven."

"That's wonderful. I guess we have something in common. I mean, besides being Christians. My father was a preacher. He and my mother are in Nigeria doing missionary work now. I'm Kaylee Pierce."

"Drew Richards."

Kaylee stepped closer, "So, what are you reading, what part?"

"First Samuel, I just finished chapter seventeen."

"Ah, the account of David and Goliath. One of my favorite verses is from that chapter."

"Really, which one?"

"Verse twenty-nine. David's response to Eliab, what have I done, is there not a cause?"

Impressive. Apparently, Kaylee Pierce knew her Bible just as well as the law.

Drew said, "You, uh..., your church, you guys were on Huron last night, right? In front of the abortion clinic."

Kaylee's mouth opened. Her expression donned a hint of suspicion.

"I pass that way when I get off work."

"I see," Kaylee's smile returned. "Yeah, um..., we try to take a few days a month to meet there, do what we can to raise awareness and to help."

"So, that's your cause, then? You know, your verse, I mean."

Kaylee laughed, said "It is, among other things. I mean, our ultimate cause is to give the gospel. Abortion, hunger, homelessness, these are just symptoms of our greater need, and that's to have our sins forgiven and have a right relationship with God through the Lord Jesus."

"You sound like my grandfather," Drew said.

Kaylee scoffed, "Is that a bad thing?"

Her hair was in a pony tail. A few loose strands hung in her face. Her smile held.

Drew replied, "Not at all."

Kaylee appeared flattered by his approval.

"So, are you a nurse? You're wearing scrubs."

"Oh, yes, Rocktown Central, Mother Baby Unit."

"Should have known." Drew grinned, said, "The other night, at the clinic, you were really giving those officers a run for their money. The way you were reciting the first amendment, thought you might be a lawyer."

The back of Kaylee's hand, the one holding the tracts, went to her mouth and her face colored. She said, "You saw that?"

Drew closed the Bible, placed it in his duffle, said, "Sure did. Happened as I was passing. Pretty impressive stuff. So, were you ever in law school?"

"Hardly. Most of what I know, I learned from my grand dad. Let's just say he's a huge advocate of the constitution. I guess, in his line of work, he has to be."

"What's his line of work?"

"Journalist. Since my parents are out of the country, I spend a lot of time with him. He's a stubborn old man, but his hearts in the right place. And, he loves the Lord."

Drew hummed acknowledgment, sipped his water.

Kaylee said, "So, what about you? From

around here?"

A homeless man on the other side of the park ate from a sack provided by one of the church members. The play area next to him sat rotted and rusted. Behind him, past the heavy flow of traffic from the bike path, the river hardly moved, apathetic to the activity around it. Kaylee stared at him with patient eyes. He said, "No, only been here a couple weeks."

"Really, where you are from?"

"Minnesota."

"Okay, so, do you have family here?"

Drew took another sip of his water, said, "No. Probably be leaving as soon as my job ends."

Kaylee glanced around the park, said, "What do you do?"

"You sure ask a lot of questions."

She shrugged, "Blame my grand dad."

Drew grinned, shook his head. He liked her. He liked her a lot. He said, "It's nothing, some manual labor."

"Do you have a church home?"

Drew paused; let his attention again drift to the river. He said, "I suppose I do. In Minnesota. Guess you could say they're leaving a light on for me."

"Well then, Mr. Richards. Why don't you be my guest at my church tomorrow? Sounds like you could use the fellowship."

Drew didn't answer, started to finish his water, noticed Kaylee's expectant stare. Apparently, she wasn't joking.

Drew said, "I don't know about that, I mean, I haven't been..."

Kaylee interrupted, "Look, all believers need to be in church under the preaching of God's word and to encourage one other to keeping fighting the good fight. I'm sure your grandfather taught you that." She went on, quoted several Bible references, in making her point.

As reluctant as Drew was to putting himself in a position where people might start asking questions, he couldn't resist the wisdom of Kaylee's argument. She really would have made a great lawyer. He agreed to go.

"Great. Service starts at nine. I'll be waiting at the doors. Can I text you the address?"

"No cell."

"Oh, sorry. I just assumed..."

"It's okay. Don't really have a need for one."

Kaylee frowned, handed him a tract, said, "Address is on back." She glanced at her watch, "I've got to go. My shift starts in an hour. See you tomorrow?"

"I'll be there," Drew said.

Kaylee started towards her group, turned, said, "I didn't think you were homeless...when I offered you lunch. I just thought you looked like you could use a friend."

She walked away. Drew hoped he wasn't making a mistake.

CHAPTER SIX

It was early evening when the bell above the door to Max's Corner Mart clanked alerting Drew's entrance. The clerk behind the register, possibly in his sixties, glanced at Drew with as much interest as he might have had toward gutter trash before returning to the magazine on the counter. The store was quiet, empty of customers. Drew snatched a basket, wasted no time filling it with necessities he needed for the week.

Reaching for a gallon of milk, Drew heard the bell clank again, followed by rough talk, thick with vulgarities, and cruel jesting. The mirror hanging in the corner revealed three of them; all early twenties, and all looking like street riff-raff. They were in the store for several minutes. That's how long it took for one of them to stroll over to the register and ask for a pack of cigarettes while the other two made quick to the liquor aisle. By the time the clerk turned, reached for the smokes and started ringing them up, they'd returned to meet their friend, the gut of their jackets a bit more pronounced than when they'd entered. Drew approached the counter just as the door shut behind them and the store became quiet again.

The old man rang up Drew's groceries, announced the total, and started bagging. He kept his gaze on his task, didn't or wouldn't look up.

Didn't matter, Drew told himself, wasn't his problem. Then why was his hand at his side balled up so tight he thought his nails would break skin? He didn't stick around to contemplate, just paid the man, snatched up the bag, milk inside, disturbed the overhead bell and left.

The wind had picked up and a haze of rain shaded the sky to his left. Thunder rattled. A storm was coming.

CHAPTER SEVEN

Kaylee waited at the doors just like she'd promised when Drew arrived, via local bus, at New Creation Baptist Church. The parking lot was three quarters full of various vehicles, some old, some new. The church itself was modest sized, newer in make, but still held to the traditional look; complete with a steeple and topped by a plain, white cross that, despite hard winds from last night's storm, stood prominent in the glare of the morning sunshine.

"Glad you could make it," Kaylee said. She was dressed in a floral patterned sundress. Her hair was pulled back in an elegant, twisting bun. A broad smile covered her face. She seemed to glow. Drew was sure his smile wouldn't be as illuminating but he offered one anyway and then followed Kaylee inside to a foyer crowded with people and booming with chatter.

After Kaylee introduced Drew to several of her 'church family', as she referred to them as, she said, "I wish you could meet my grand dad but he won't be back until this afternoon."

Drew nodded, tried not to show his relief. Although Kaylee's 'church family' seemed genuinely glad he was there, their questions, so far, had been superficial. He was thankful for that. But, by the way Kaylee had described her grand dad, Drew didn't think his questions would be so...surface level.

When the service started, Kaylee offered Drew to sit next to her in a pew towards the center of the sanctuary. The proceedings were similar to Drew's church back in Minnesota. The hymnals they sang from were filled with 'old hymns of the faith', as Drew's grandfather liked to call them, and Drew had grown up singing. As the service progressed, Drew found himself very comfortable around this body of believers, was glad he'd come.

The preaching was expository, verse by verse, line upon line. And, although up in years, the preacher spoke clearly with passion and conviction. The text he'd directed the congregation to turn their Bibles to was John18:40-'not this man, but Barabbas.'

As he preached, Drew's heart stirred. Jesus had been rejected by his own people. The one who had come to save them, they had crucified and chose rather to free a robber, a murderer...*a pedophile!*

Drew was cut to the marrow. He recalled the passage in Hebrews where it talked about Jesus being tempted like as we are yet without sin. Drew considered the injustice that he, himself, had suffered; the rejection, the accusations, the loss of his job, and Jen, and two years of his life. Jesus had endured far more and on a far greater, more infinite level. Yet Jesus was without sin before His rejection and after. He hadn't become bitter or angry, hadn't turned his back on those he loved. He endured what he did for those He loved.

The preacher lifted his voice, "It is the will of God to conform all of His children into the image of Christ. He uses suffering and the rejection of this world to do so. And so, when we are faced with so great an ordeal, we should look to Christ as our example, our hope, and our strength."

He ended the service by allotting a few minutes of silent reflection and prayer.

Drew bowed his head, asked the Lord's forgiveness for having harbored bitterness in his heart for so long and sought wisdom in moving forward. He ended his prayer in the Lord's name, opened his eyes, saw Kaylee finishing her prayer. Apparently, the Lord was speaking to her heart, as well. When she looked up, her face was aglow with a peaceful contentment. There was no pretense of awkwardness. Their Heavenly Father had worked in their hearts. Drew felt very fortunate. The tender smile that Kaylee gave him, told him she felt the same.

Back in the foyer, after most of the congregation had left, Kaylee introduced Drew to the preacher, who she referred to as Pastor Williams. She offered to the Pastor as much as Drew had mentioned of himself, that he was a believer, new to the area, but would only be in Rocktown for a short while. Pastor Williams responded cordially, giving Drew a firm handshake, and telling him the church was honored that he had visited.

Kaylee's cell bleeped. Apologizing, she excused herself.

"So, Drew, if you don't mind me asking, where are you going when you leave Rocktown? I might be able to recommend a good church in that area."

"I appreciate that, Pastor, but..." Drew stuffed his hands in his pockets, looked up and took in a breath. The extent of God's grace working in him flooded his emotions. He resisted welling up, said, "Don't think I'll need it. Up until just a little while ago, I didn't have any idea where I was heading, but..." again he took a breath, couldn't believe what he was about to say, "I think I'm going back to my hometown. I have a church there. Lot of people praying for me. They'll be happy I'm back, I'm sure."

Pastor Williams looked pleased, put a hand on Drew's shoulder, said, "Glad to hear that. As long as you're following the Lord, you can be assured you're heading in the right direction."

An elderly woman cut in, said there was a matter that required the Pastor's attention. Pastor Williams excused himself. Drew caught sight of Kaylee in a small office at the back of the foyer. A plaque on the partially opened door read- Kaylee Pierce Outreach Coordinator. Kaylee was still on her cell. She seemed distressed. Drew watched her snatch a pen from the desk she stood over and jot something down on a notepad. Ripping off the page, she shoved her cell and the paper into her handbag and then exited the room.

"Drew, I'm sorry, I have to leave. Something important has come up. I wanted to...If your still in town next Sunday, come visit again. My grand dad will be here. I'd love for you to meet him."

"Sure thing," Drew said. "Is everything alright?"

Kaylee started to say something, hesitated, then offered, "Yes, everything's fine. I just don't have time to explain right now. I'm sorry." She paused again, looked like she wanted to say more but didn't. She turned and hurried out of the church.

CHAPTER EIGHT

On Monday, Drew put in a few extra hours to finish the job at the supply yard. He collected his final pay, said his goodbyes and made fast tracks back to his apartment. It was dark out when he got there. After a shower and a quick dinner, he kicked back on the couch, remote in hand, in time to catch the ten o'clock news. He wasn't particularly interested in what was happening around Rocktown. He'd be leaving at the end of the week when his rent was up. What he was interested in was the weather-especially in Minnesota.

By the end of the opening highlights, his eyelids felt like bags of sand and he fought to stay awake as the anchor woman went over the evening's top story. It wasn't the 'what' of the details but the 'who', that snapped him to an upright position like a longhorn out of a bull pen. Tragedy, crime, and death

permeated this town like the stench of rotting fish. He'd
smelled it from the moment he first stepped off the
bus; a familiar aroma, the same as most dying cities in
the mid west that he'd passed through. A woman in
critical condition found at the bottom of a bridge, he
would have chalked up as a sad but hard statistic of
living in the armpit of America. That is, if he hadn't
known her. But he did know her. The news woman
identified her as local resident, Kaylee Pierce.

Drew sat at the edge of the sofa, leaned
toward the television. His mouth gaped in disbelief as
he took in the details. Apparently, investigators had
found no evidence of foul play and were treating the
incident as an unfortunate accident. The news woman
reported that Mrs. Pierce was being treated in the ICU
at Rocktown Central. And then, the weekly weather
coverage began. Drew was no longer interested. He
killed the television. No noise came through the
window. The town was silent. His first impulse was to
throw on some clothes and beat feet over to the
hospital. That's exactly what he did.

Rocktown Central was eight miles from his
apartment. It was just after midnight when he arrived.
He entered around back through the emergency
department, being that normal visiting hours had long
since ended and the front entrance was now locked.

Passing an armed security guard and a
waiting room full of Rocktown statistics, Drew went

straight to the check-in window, explained why he was
there and was directed to a set of elevators that he took
to the third floor.

The ICU was lined by glass walled rooms,
three to each side. Curtains behind the glass were
drawn for privacy. The nurses station sat dead center. It
was occupied by two females in caricatured scrubs,
each with stethoscopes draped around their necks. One
looked young enough to be fresh out of nursing school.
The other, on the verge of retirement. They sat engaged
in whispered chatter and snickered over something on a
cell phone. Drew stepped up to the desk. The nurses
stifled their giggles, the cell vanished.

"Can I help you?" The younger nurse asked.

"I'm here for Kaylee Pierce. Can you tell me
how she's doing?"

"Sure." She picked up a clipboard, started
leafing through charts. Her I.D read Julia Reynolds. The
photo looked recent. The elder nurse, who'd spun
around in her padded swivel and was clicking away at a
keyboard, offered, "She's the one from Mother Baby,
bed nine."

"Yep! Got her right here. Let's see, pelvic
fracture, a couple broken ribs, head trauma and internal
bleeding. She really was in bad shape when they
brought her in. But, she's stable now. She still hasn't
woke from her coma, though. We won't be able to

know the extent of damage from the head trauma till then."

"Can I see her?" Drew asked.

"Are you family?"

"No, just a friend."

"I'm sorry, but only immediate family are allowed in patient rooms after visiting hours. You'll have to come back in the morning. We do have a waiting area through those doors."

Her sugary tone made the option seem almost enjoyable. Almost. But, it was better than huffing it back to his apartment just to turn around again. Besides, stretched out in a cushioned arm chair wouldn't be the worst place he'd ever slept.

He started for the doors. The elder nurse swiveled, raised out of her chair, said, "Hold on a sec."

Her I.D read Sue Baker. Her photo wasn't as recent as Julia's. Twenty to thirty years, not as recent.

"Jules, Kaylee's one of us. Her parents can't get back to the States for another week, visa issues, so I think a friend is exactly what she needs right now." Nurse Sue looked at Drew, said, "Sometimes when a coma patient hears a familiar voice it can help bring them out of it. You can have a few minutes if you'd like. And if you don't mind, try talking to her. It just might help."

"Sure thing," Drew said.

Still smiling, still sugary, Jules pointed, "Last room on your right."

Kaylee's head was wrapped in thick gauze. A tube went up her nose and there were several IV's taped to her arm. Monitors beeped and their screens pulsated with activity.

Drew went to her bedside. She looked peaceful, like she was napping. Her breathing was smooth and even. Maybe the nurse was right. Maybe Kaylee would be able to hear him if he spoke to her. But what could he say? He hardly knew her. Still, she'd been kind to him, helped him, befriended him. He had to say something. He owed her that much and a lot more.

He said, "Hi Kaylee, It's Drew Richards, the guy you invited to church. I wanted to thank you for talking with me, you know, at the park the other day. And, for having me at your church. It meant a lot. More than you know." He paused, cleared his throat. It'd been a long time since he'd been this open with anyone, even himself. He said, "I'm going back to Minnesota Friday, face some things I've been running from."

Kaylee's hand lay at her side. Drew took it in his, said, "I don't know why God allowed what He did in my life, but I know He loves me and He's working it for my good and I don't understand why this happened to you, either. But, I know we just have to trust the Lord, Kaylee. He has a plan and a purpose for everything. Somehow He'll work this for your good."

"Times up." Nurse Sue was at the door. She glanced at Kaylee, offered a smile.

Drew squeezed Kaylee's hand, was about to let go, when he noticed something odd on her wrist.

Nurse Sue must have noticed his expression. She stepped next to him, said, "Nothing to be concerned about, just bruising from the fall."

Drew frowned, said, "Maybe, but look at this." He traced the marks with his finger. "See the pattern. It almost looks like someone had ahold of her wrist. Like they were trying to restrain her."

All semblance of politeness faded from Nurse Sue's face. Apparently, she wasn't fond of having her twenty to thirty years of nursing expertise challenged. But, Drew had some expertise of his own, too. He'd been to more domestic violence calls than he could remember, and the marks left on many of those victims hands and arms closely resembled the marks on Kaylee. He said, "Look at her nails, and the scrapes on her hand."

Nurse Sue planted her fists on her hips. Her

chin lifted. She said, "Now hold on, Mr. Richards. I think you're getting way off track here and I don't like where you're heading. The police have already said it wasn't anything like that. Kaylee fell and that's all there is to it." She stared hard for a moment, then softened, said, "Look, I understand it's a tragic and senseless thing that happened. And it's natural to want to make sense of it, to find some meaning, or someone to blame. But, there's no meaning. Nobody did this to her. It just happened. It was an accident. And you have to accept that. When Kaylee wakes up, hopefully she can tell us exactly what happened. How she slipped or whatever. But, until then Mr. Richards, you're not helping anyone by turning this into something it isn't."

Was that what he was doing? It was true; the marks could have come from the fall. The authorities had determined it so. Nurse Sue was obviously convinced. Who was he to question their judgment? After all, he wasn't a cop any more. Kaylee still looked peaceful. The room was quiet except for the steady, rhythmic bleeping of the monitors.

Nurse Sue said, "I've got rounds to do. Really, I think it's time for you to leave. Come back in the morning, Mr. Richards. Who knows, maybe Kaylee'll be awake by then. Like Jules said, you can stay in the waiting area if you'd like."

Drew nodded and then left Kaylee's room. Nurse Jules was still at the station and back on her cell.

Her cell! The call! Kaylee had been clearly troubled about something while on her phone. Something important had come up, she'd said. Was it just coincidence that she'd been found the next day under a bridge? And, with marks on her hands and wrists consistent with being in a struggle. Maybe. But he didn't put much stock in maybes or coincidences. And as far as making this into something it wasn't... There was only one way to know for sure and he owed it to Kaylee to find out.

He didn't go to waiting area, took the elevator to the main floor. He needed more information and had a good idea where to get it.

CHAPTER NINE

The Rocktown Police department was four stories of glass, mortar, stone and steel and ran the entire block of Fifth and Charles. Drew went inside, was met by two officers manning a metal detecting unit. He fished his apartment key from his jeans, tossed it in a basket and stepped through without any disturbance. After retrieving his key, he crossed the lobby to the attending officer at the window and asked to speak with the detective who'd worked Kaylee's case. The officer made a call, said someone would be with him shortly.

Several minutes later, Drew was met by Officer Harris, a beat cop, exceptionally tall with shoulders enough to even him out. He escorted Drew to an elevator and up to the second floor. When the elevator opened, Drew was a bit surprised. Unlike the Detective Unit in Wakefield, which consisted of an entire open floor crammed with a mess of desks and cubicles, Drew stared down a wide carpeted hallway. Ornate mahogany doors lined either side. At the end of the hall dust particles floated in sunlight streaming through a large single window. The floor was silent, serine like.

Officer Harris directed Drew to the first door on the left. A name plate hung on the door- Detective R.D. Powers. Drew went in.

Powers was seated behind a high end desk, looked to be in his early fifties, wore a standard button up, loose tie. He was clean, well groomed. His hair was slicked back, dark, with a shock of grey at the sides. His smile was cordial enough but his eyes were hard, ice blue, and the lines around them told Drew he was no push over. The detective motioned to the chair in front of his desk. Drew sat.

Powers said, "So, Mr. Richards, Officer Lynn said you had some concerns about the Pierce incident. How can I help?"

"I heard about Kaylee over the news. Didn't give much detail. I was hoping you could tell me a little more about what happened?"

"Not much to tell, really. Got a call from a pedestrian yesterday afternoon, someone walking their dog, happened to see Mrs. Pierce lying near the tracks at the bottom of the Morton Street Bridge. From the forensics, she'd probably been there nearly twenty four hours. We found her shoulder bag. Nothing seemed to have been taken. So, she wasn't robbed. No evidence of sexual assault or anything of that nature," Powers leaned back, locked his hands behind his head, "So, either Mrs. Pierce slipped and fell, and believe me, it's possible. The railings on that bridge are flimsy and low and it wouldn't be the first time someone's gone over out there. Frankly, it's not the safest area to be in. Everything west of Brook road is old and falling apart. All kinds of mishaps in that part of the city. So, she most likely went over the rail by accident or..." He sat up, "No offense, but there's always the possibility she put herself over the rail. Jumped. It wouldn't be the first time that's happened out there, either."

"I can assure you, Detective, that's not the case. Kaylee isn't like that."

"I see." Powers stared at his hands like he was contemplating something, said, "So, you must know Mrs. Pierce pretty well then. Are you related? Boyfriend?"

"No, nothing like that. Just a friend."

"And how long have you and Mrs. Pierce been friends?"

"Not long."

"I see." Powers leaned back again, "You

wouldn't happen to know why Mrs. Pierce was in that vicinity, would you?"

"No idea."

Powers made a face like it really didn't matter anyway, said, "Well, whatever the situation, I'm sure when Mrs. Pierce wakes up we'll get a better understanding of what happened. But, I'm afraid that's about I can tell you for now. So, if there's nothing else, I've got work to do."

"Actually, there is. I saw Kaylee last night at the hospital. She had..."

Powers cell chimed. He held up his hand, answered.

Drew sat back as much as the arm chair would allow. The walnut top of Powers desk was dust free, neat and tidy. Several papers were stacked in the center. To one side, behind a tin of pens, was a book. It lay flat and wrapped in plastic, hadn't been opened. Drew read the spine; Beginners guide to the Wiccan religion. Taped on the plastic, on the cover, was a note. Drew couldn't make out what it said from where he sat, but he could make out the signature scribbled at the bottom of the page-Sam.

Powers snatched up the book.

"Research," he said, tucking it away in a

drawer. He was off the phone. "You were saying you saw Mrs. Pierce?"

"That's right. I noticed some bruising on her wrist. Looked a lot like grip marks. Her nails and knuckles were scuffed too, like she'd been in a confrontation."

Powers stared level, said, "Mr. Richards, Mrs. Pierce took a twenty five foot free fall right smack into solid earth. I'd say that's a bit of a confrontation, wouldn't you?"

"I understand Detective, but I was with Kaylee Sunday morning. Went to church with her. She got a call right after service and then left real quick. Said something had come up. She seemed like something was wrong."

"Did she say what it was about? Where she was going?"

"No."

Powers reclined again, scratched his chin, "So, you say you were with Mrs. Pierce Sunday morning. Can anyone collaborate that you two didn't leave together?"

Drew tensed, wasn't sure where Powers was heading with the question, said, "There were several people still there when I left. I'm sure someone can vouch for that. You think I had something to do with what happened to Kaylee. "

"Relax, Mr. Richards, just trying to get the facts." He went quiet for a moment, then said, "Look, you said so yourself, you've only known Mrs. Pierce a short while. And, if you're not her boyfriend, maybe someone else is. Maybe he's the jealous type. Maybe it was him on the phone threatening to end it because he didn't like her being out with another guy, that guy being you. And maybe she goes to see him and they do get into a scuffle. She tries to leave. He grabs her arm. She pulls away, goes out to Morton Street. Either by her own doing or by accident finds herself going over the bridge. You see what I'm getting at?"

Unfortunately, Drew had a good idea, and even if he hadn't, Powers went on to spell it out, make his point clear. He said, "Even if the bruises were made by someone grabbing Mrs. Pierce arm, it doesn't mean foul play's involved. We did a thorough investigation and there just isn't any evidence to support that assumption. I know you care about your friend, I get it. But, why don't you leave the police work to the police. Now, like I said, unless you got something else for me, I've got to get back to solving real crimes. You can show yourself out."

Drew did.

CHAPTER TEN

The Morton Street Bridge was on the far west side of town, roughly ten miles from the police station. Drew got directions from the attendant on the way out of the precinct, caught the city bus for eight of those miles, walked the last two.

Powers was right. The area surrounding the bridge was nothing more than old brick, sagging fire escapes and rusted smokestacks. Graffiti decorated every block. The pavement was crumbly and pot holed. Even the trees seemed diseased and dead. There was no traffic, no people, no activity, and no good reason for Kaylee to have come out there. Nor himself. Powers might have been hard-nosed and arrogant, but he seemed competent. And, as much as it pained Drew to admit it, the detective had a point. Police work was for the police to do and he wasn't the police, not anymore.

So, why was he standing on the east side of the bridge looking down at train tracks. He didn't have an answer.

The bridge itself was a decrepit sight of weathered cement and rusted iron. It was two-laned, ran about fifty feet end to end. The railing, which covered the entire span of the bridge on either side, was a single rod with support bars running vertically and spaced about every ten feet. It stood maybe three feet high, exceptionally low for a bridge rail. Powers had said as much.

Drew gripped the railing, yanked on it. It moved. Enough, that if someone leaned against it, unaware of its condition, it was possible, probable even, that the person would have tumbled over.

Drew checked the other side with the same result, imagined the fear Kaylee must have experienced going over. He swallowed hard, stared again at the tracks below. The ground, mostly rock and dirt, seemed undisturbed. That made sense. Post forensics would have already been out to clean and sanitize. There'd be no crime scene tape because, according to Powers, there had been no crime. In which case, Drew didn't think he'd be breaking any laws if he went down to have a look around.

After twenty minutes or so, and only finding a small stain in the dirt, which may or may not have been Kaylees blood, Drew slumped against the base of one of the iron pillars that supported the bridge. Powers had called it right. There was nothing there. Why Kaylee would have come out to such a remote section of town, Drew had no idea. He also had no clue as to who had called her Sunday morning or what was said that had caused her to leave in such a hurry. Was that even relevant? He didn't have an answer. Maybe there was no answer. Maybe, Nurse Sue had also called it right, too. Maybe he was trying to find a reason for such a senseless event. Maybe he did want someone to blame.

Drew picked up a stone, whipped it at the tracks, watched it ricochet. The act reminded him of skipping rocks across Marlin Pond with his grandfather. He thought about his home town, and his plans to leave Rocktown on Friday. He wondered if he should postpone, stick around until Kaylee was out of her coma. She was his friend, even more so, a sister in Christ. But, what if she didn't wake up for a month...a year? What if she didn't wake up at all? Drew prayed.

When he finished, thunder didn't rattle, the heavens didn't open, and the audible voice of God didn't instruct him on what to do. But, he was confident the Lord had heard him and would grant him the wisdom he sought. He figured the best course of action for now was to go back to his apartment and get some rest. He hadn't slept much last night. He'd visit Kaylee in the morning.

Wanting one last whip at the tracks, he inspected the ground for an ideal skipper, caught sight of something else. It lay next to the tracks, just outside the reach of the darker shadows. It was round, larger than a silver dollar, and black. Definitely, not a rock. He picked it up. Hard plastic. A lid or cap of some sort. Turning it over, he read the words- Nikon.

Drew heard voices, looked up, saw four men approaching. Local gangbangers, he surmised from their appearance. Besides sideways caps and bandanas, they all wore wicked grins of intent. They didn't rush in, just spread out and steadily came at him.

CHAPTER ELEVEN

The gangbanger in the middle, the one with muscles like he'd done a stretch in the pen, said, "What you doing out here, man?"

Drew didn't answer but the guys buddy's sure seemed amused by the question. Something else, they kept glancing past him. Drew reeled, was sucker punched. He staggered, managed to stay on his feet, took another blow to the head. He fell. The gangbangers charged. How many, he wasn't sure. Five, seven, ten. He tried to move, to get to feet, but they swarmed on him like angry wasps, kicking and punching and stomping him down until all he could do was ball up into a defensive position and endure the attack.

The beatdown ended with Drew splayed out on his back and being manipulated like a rag doll by a couple extra kicks to the ribs. He felt hands pat him down, his wallet lifted. It landed on his chest a moment later, fifty bucks lighter, he was sure.

A switchblade flicked. One of the gangbangers moved toward him. Drew prepared for the worst.

Another gangbanger, the one with the muscles, stepped between them, said something. The other backed off. Muscles turned, stood over Drew, said, "Got some advice dog, leave town cause next time we ain't playin' so nice."

A siren squawked. Someone yelled, "Hey! What's going on down there?"

The gangbangers fled.

Fifteen minutes later, Drew sat at the back of an ambulance atop the bridge giving his statement to one of Rocktowns finest. The paramedic tending to his ribs, said, "Sure you don't want to come to the hospital and get this checked out?"

"I'll be alright," Drew said, wincing as he pulled his shirt down, "I don't think anything's broken. Just gonna be sore for a few days."

"I'll say. Got to hand it to you, how you managed to come out of that with just some cuts and bruising, you gotta be one tough hombre."

"He certainly is."

Powers stepped out from around the side of the ambulance, his hands shoved in the pockets of his chinos. "Led the Wakefield Wildcats to State two years in a row, received a purple heart while doing a four year stint in the Marines. After that, five years on the Wakefield Police Department."

The paramedic looked impressed. Detective Powers, not so much.

The paramedic handed Drew a release to sign, said it was standard protocol since Drew was refusing the trip to the hospital, then, shut the back doors, and headed towards the front of the vehicle. Powers kept his gaze locked on Drew. The ambulance pulled away. Power's Sedan was parked on the opposite side of the bridge. Both men faced each other.

"So, why didn't you tell me you were a cop?"

"I'm not."

Powers laughed, although clearly not amused. He said, "What are you doing at my crime scene?"

"So now what happened to Kaylee is a crime."

"You're a real funny guy, Richards." And then serious as a pitbull, he said, "Answer the question."

Drew said nothing.

"Look, I'm not in the mood. You start talking or I'm taking you in."

"On what charge?"

Powers hands were out of his pockets. "For ticking me off! For obstruction! For anything I can think of that'll have you sitting in a jail cell for the next month!"

Drew weighed Powers threat, decided it was legit, said, "Out for a walk. No crime in that."

Powers jaw tightened. A vein throbbed at his temple. Suddenly, he relaxed.

"Look Richards, I checked you out, read your file. I know what happened. And, I get it. You got a raw deal. Liberal judge decides to make an example out of you. Two years up state. And for what? Smacking around some scum bag pedophile. Sheesh! A cop can't even do his job anymore."

Powers conjured up a pack of cigarettes from his breast pocket, lit one up.

"So, how long you been out, a year, year and a half?"

Drew's throat tightened. And not just from the smoke.

Powers took another long drag, blew it in Drew's direction.

"So, what are you doing here, Richards?"

"I told you, walking."

"No, not here," Powers snapped, "I mean here, in Rocktown. You got friends or relatives?"

The tracks stretched into the distance, faded around a bend.

"No, nothing like that. Just passing through. Planned on catching a bus out of here Friday."

"Well now, that's the best news I heard all week. A piece of advice, stick to that plan."

Drew scoffed.

"Something funny?" Powers asked.

Drew said, "You sound a lot like the guys who jumped me. Gave me the same advice."

Powers flicked his cigarette over the bridge, "Look, I don't know what those punks said to you. And personally, I don't care. You shouldn't have been out here in the first place. What I do know is I got an ex-cop, whose also an ex-con, walking my streets like he's still wearing a badge, trying to solve things that don't need solved, and sticking his nose where it doesn't belong."

"It isn't like that."

"No? Well, it sure looks like that to me. And the last thing I need is having to explain to my captain why I got another body in the ICU. You get what I'm saying, Richards?"

"Yeah, I get you. But I can handle myself."

"Yeah, I can tell. Come on, I'm giving you a ride back to whatever hole your staying at."

"I think I'll walk."

The vein in Powers temple throbbed again. He said, "I'm not asking, I'm telling you, get in the car. You don't want to try me. I'll lock you away and have your paper work so shuffled in the system, you'll be pulling gray hairs out of your ears before you ever get an arraignment. Am I making myself clear?"

The guy definitely had grit. Drew liked that about him. Nothing else. He replied, "Crystal."

"Good. Now get in the car. And Richards, you be on that bus come Friday. If I so much as hear your name before then, I'm coming down on you hard, ex-cop or not."

CHAPTER TWELVE

It was late afternoon when Drew packed his belongings into a duffle, locked up his apartment for the last time and returned the key to the manager's office. He asked to use the phone, called the bus station to confirm departure times and check the cost of a non coach into Wakefield. It was comfortably under what he'd stashed away in the back of his sock drawer, which hadn't been in his wallet when he'd been mugged. It was for that possibility he'd started the habit of not having all his cash with him at one time.

The bus depot was located several blocks from the hospital. Drew figured he had time to pop in, see how Kaylee was doing, say goodbye whether she was awake or not. His ribs were still sore, though not nearly as much as they'd been. The bruising had started to yellow and the last two days of ice pack treatments had helped considerably. It'd also given him time to think, to do some in-depth Bible reading and pray.

He entered through the front of the hospital this time, made his way past the reception area, and took an elevator to the third floor. He exited into a hallway. The ICU was on the other side of a set of doors at the end of the hall. To his right, was a large waiting area. There were several plush couches, a few chairs, some end tables, soft lighting. The room Nurse Jules had suggested to him the other night. For all intent and purposes, it looked quite comfy. The far side of the room opened up into another hall that ran in either direction.

Drew went to the doors, pressed the intercom. A buzzer sounded and he went in. A nurse, blonde, hurried from around the nurses station and disappeared into a patients room. She, nor the two other hospital staff standing at the far side of the ward doing report, paid him any mind. Shift change, possibly. He didn't wait around to be helped, showed himself to Kaylee's room.

The door was partially open. A petite, dark haired nurse stood at far side of Kaylees bed. Her back was to him and she appeared to be doing something with the lines of the I.V bag. Kaylee was still attached to monitors, still looked to be in a coma.

Drew entered. The nurse turned. She was

middle aged and pretty.

"Sorry, is it alright to visit for a few?" Drew said.

The nurse gave him a polite smile, hurried past to leave. When she did, her shoulder smacked into him. Two things happened, almost simultaneously. One, Drew caught his breath from the jolt to his ribs, almost dropped his duffle. Two, the nurses hand yanked out of the pocket of her smock. Something fell to the floor. Drew heard it bounce against the tile and then roll under the bed.

"Sorry," he apologized for the second time and bent down to retrieve the object. It was a glass vial of some sort, about the size of an aspirin bottle and a quarter full of clear liquid. It had a generic label with medical jargon that Drew was unfamiliar with. He stood. The nurse was gone. He stepped out the room, hoping to catch her. The two staff, across the ward, were still doing report. The blonde nurse, the one that had buzzed him in, was back behind the nurses station speaking with a doctor, giggling and playing with her hair. The nurse who'd dropped the vial, was nowhere to be seen.

Kaylee's monitors suddenly blurted to life. Drew spun around. Kaylee jerked and twitched. Within seconds, the doctor barged in, the other staff behind him. He demanded stats and gave orders for measured cc's of treatments.

"It's not working. Her heart rates still spiking!" the blonde nurse said.

Drew looked at the vial in his hand. The doctor must have noticed.

"What is that?" he snapped.

Drew didn't know, held out the vial in his palm. The doctor snatched it up, read the label. Hard concern lined his face. He shouted out several more orders in which the nurses complied and within a few moments the monitors started quieting, returning to rhythm.

Everyone stared at Drew. He recognized their expressions. They were same kind of faces that had accused him, convicted him, and had destroyed his life.

"I didn't…" He took a step back.

"Call security!" The doctor said.

Drew ran.

A nurse was entering the ward through the double doors. Drew barreled past, almost knocking her over. He still held his duffle, halted at the elevator, repeatedly jabbed at the down button. He looked back. The doctor was at the double doors, a security guard next to him. The elevator sounded. Drew started to rush in, but stopped. Detective Powers stood in front of him. Their eyes locked. Powers must have read Drew's panic because his face got real dark real fast. He reached out, tried to apprehend Drew by the shirt.

Drew shot to his left, darted through the waiting area and into the corridor on the other side. Spotting the fire exit, he tore open the door, raced into the stairwell and flew down the steps. All the while, he gritted his teeth against hot stabs of pain from his bruised ribs.

Powers pursued, yelled for him to stop just as Drew raced into the ground floor lobby. Weaving through the mass of staff and visitors, Drew made it to the front doors and darted out into the parking lot.

Within minutes, he was in the shadows of an alleyway, hunched over, gasping for air, his duffle on the pavement beside him. He was confident Powers hadn't pursued. He was just as confident the detective would be putting out an APB any minute, if he hadn't already. He was a fugitive. Every cop in the city would be looking for him. Attempted murder. That's what they'd tell Powers. And, Powers would believe them. He already had it out for him. He'd made that clear. There was no use trying to explain.

"Oh God, what do I do?" he breathed. There was no answer, no feeling of peace this time, just cold assurance that he had to move.

With no clear destination in mind other than as far from the area as he could get, Drew picked up his duffle and stepped out of the alley into the cold breeze of the approaching night.

CHAPTER THIRTEEN

The train yard was as desolate as the view from Gus's supply house had suggested. The bordering chain-link was about eight feet tall, weathered, and crowned with three tiered barbwire. Drew found a section missing the barb, tossed over his duffle. Moving slow, careful not to jar his ribs, he climbed over himself, and then sprinted to the nearest box car.

The door was open, slid completely to one side, revealing the interior. Besides a few patches of rust, the floor was clean and intact. Drew threw up his duffle, climbed in, and tried the door. It offered some resistance, but the rollers were functional and the door squealed shut. He left it cracked, though, not wanting to chance it latching. That's all he needed was to be locked in a metal cage for the rest of his life. Yet, that's exactly what he was facing.

Resting his duffle against the wall, he slumped down. The moonlight through the crack was enough that Drew could see his hands trembling. And, despite the cool winds that had starting blowing, he was sweating hard. He took a breath, calmed himself, and contemplated his options. There were only two.

One was to go on as he was, a fugitive, live underground, and off grid. Pretty much like he'd been living for the past two years. Cash jobs, no phone, no accounts or anything that could be traced or tracked. He'd have to change his appearance, score a fake I.D. Not too difficult. Not with the knowledge he had. He'd been on both sides, knew the angles, how the streets operated and how the badges worked. He could stay a free man until he was old and gray.

But, that option was carnal, rooted in fear. It was fear that had caused him to run in the first place. He was aware of that now. He also was aware that the option was a lie. Not that he couldn't evade capture. That was true. But, he wouldn't be free. God had spoken to him through Pastor William's message, had opened his eyes to the fact that he may have been out of prison for the last two years but he hadn't been free. Afterwards, all he'd wanted was to go home, be with his family, try and make up for lost time, go fishing with his grandfather, sit under his preaching. And, to see Marcus and Deena, meet their kid. He didn't know if it was a boy or girl, hadn't so much as called in all this time. If he ran, he'd never get that chance, to call, go home, none of it.

Another thing, the option was selfish. Someone had tried to kill Kaylee. The bridge wasn't an accident. The hospital must have been an attempt to finish the job. It failed. The dark haired nurse, if she was a nurse, was still out there. Neither the hospital nor the police knew anything about her. Kaylee was still in danger. If he ran, there'd be no one to help her, to protect her.

Also, going on the run was sin, simple as that. And Drew was done with sin. He'd been enslaved to it since the trial, in the gall of bitterness, as the Bible called it. And he wasn't about to let himself be ensnared again. He was well aware what the Bible taught about submitting to authorities and governments. He'd studied the principle, had it breaded into him by his family and church since he was a child. That's why he hadn't run when he was wrongly accused and sentenced to prison the first time. He'd trusted God then. Knew God had a reason and a plan for allowing Him to get locked up. Somewhere along the way his faith had faltered. But, God is faithful and had strengthened him, had given him eyes to see the truth. He wouldn't run. He'd stay free this time, even if he did go back to prison. The right thing to do was to turn himself in. And he would. But, not until he had some kind of evidence to give to Powers that proved Kaylees life was in danger and not by him. That way, the police would protect her until she came out of her coma and could tell them herself, who was after her, and why. That is, if she came out. There were no guarantees. And, there was no telling what the stuff that'd been injected into her had done. Had it made her condition worse? Drew could do nothing but hope for the best and pray.

Rain fell, slow at first, and then it picked up, sounding like a thousand angry fists beating against the roof. Drew adjusted his duffle, used it as a pillow, and started thinking about where to find the evidence he'd need to convince Powers? He'd already been to the bridge, hadn't found anything but a lens cover. It might have been irrelevant, a piece of debris. Powers hadn't mentioned a camera. Why not? It would have fit into his theory of Kaylee's fall being an accident. He could have said she was taking pictures, wasn't watching where she going, leaned too far over the rail or something like that. But he didn't. So, more than likely, Powers hadn't found a camera. That's why not. And that meant, if the lens cover wasn't just a coincidental finding, and it actually was Kaylee's, then someone had taken the camera before the police had gotten there. But why? Had Kaylee seen something or had taken pictures of something that someone was willing to kill for to keep secret. If the lens cover was Kaylee's, then it was obvious, she had. Maybe the guy's who jumped him knew something. He could go back, track them down, question them. Problem was, he couldn't remember most of them, hadn't really seen them, but he'd seen Muscles, was sure he'd recognize him. He found himself liking the idea of getting reacquainted with the big guy. Things would go down a lot different than their last rendezvous. He was sure of that. But, the likelihood of Muscles being at the bridge and hanging around alone was slim. To slim for him to chance a hike across town and possibly getting apprehended by the police.

Maybe there was something at Kaylee's residence that would give him a clue as to what was going on. That seemed a reasonable place to start. But, he didn't know Kaylee's residence. He only knew where she worked. And, he couldn't go back there. Even if he could, the hospital didn't just give out employee information. And, he doubted she'd have any personals on the Mother Baby Unit. It wasn't like nurses had their own office. But, outreach coordinators did! Offices with computers! He'd seen one on the Kaylee's desk when she was on the phone. He could look up her address online. Tomorrow was Saturday. It was probable someone would be there getting things ready for the Sunday service. He could get there early, slip in and out without being seen. He wouldn't be breaking in, not technically. The doors would be open, so there was no moral dilemma in doing so. Besides, he was trying to help Kaylee. That had to count for something.

He listened to the beating of the rain against the car and the whipping of the wind outside. After a long while, he fell asleep.

CHAPTER FOURTEEN

The morning brought dismal gray overcast and heavy winds. The rain had stopped. Drew dug through his duffle, retrieved the city map he'd picked up when first arriving in Rocktown, shoved it in his back pocket. He then threw on a hooded jacket, kept the hood up, left the train yard the same way he'd entered, minus his duffle. He left that in the car, figured he'd be returning if nothing panned out, and headed for the church.

There wasn't much traffic on the roads. The cars that did pass paid him as much attention as the puddles they sped through. A digital bank sign flashed the time-8:37. A few blocks later, he neared the church. The cross on the steeple still stood high and prominent above the neighborhood. Two cars were in the parking lot; an ancient model Plymouth, the size of an ocean liner and a silver Ford Hybrid. Neither showed any indication of being an unmarked. Not that he expected the police to be there, but he wasn't leaving anything to chance. He shot across the lot, tried the door, it opened.

The foyer was empty but someone was playing the piano in the main auditorium. Drew hurried to Kaylee's office, closed the door.

The office was a small, single squared room. The only distinguishing features were an industrial sized copier in the corner and across from it a book shelf built into the wall. It was filled with religious titles, some of which Drew recognized, classics of the faith, written by men that Drew greatly admired. He found himself impressed with Kaylee all the more. In front of the book shelf was her desk and computer. He rounded the desk, grabbed the mouse waking the monitor. A blue locked screen appeared.

Drew tensed. He hadn't figured on her computer being locked, didn't have a clue as to what the password might be. He tried the name of the church. Nothing. Typed in Kaylee's name. Same result. He then searched the items on the desk, rummaged through the drawers. They were filled with gospel tracts, pro life pamphlets, and other church literature, but nothing that indicated a password.

Suddenly, somebody spoke from just

outside the office. Drew froze, realized the piano was no longer playing. Several voices exchanged pleasantries in the foyer and commenced in conversation. He recognized one of the voices. Pastor Williams. A minute later, the conversation ended. There was silence for about thirty seconds and then the piano started again, this time joined by a male vocal.

Drew scanned the desk again; a pencil tray, notepad, and a black bound Bible.

What was it that Kaylee had said at the park? One of her favorite verses…He remembered, typed in 1st Samual 17:29. The screen remained locked. He cleared the box, typed in Is there not a cause. The blue screen vanished revealing a desktop screen of several application icons over a backdrop photo of Kaylee standing next to a gruff looking man with gray hair, a thick mustache, and sharp eyes. Kaylee and the man were both smiling. Her grand dad, Drew presumed. And then his attention was arrested by what hung around Kaylee's neck. A very expensive looking Nikon camera. His assumption had been right. The lens cap he'd found was hers. Which meant someone had taken the camera before the police arrived. But why? What was it that Kaylee had seen or had taken photos of? Drew hoped he'd have the answer soon.

He clicked the internet icon, went to the Rocktown White Pages. In the search tab, he typed in Kaylee Pierce, clicked enter. A blue ring appeared in the center of the screen, chased itself for about ten seconds, and then a list of three results showed; three Kaylee Pierce residents with their address and birthdates. One put Kaylee at age sixty seven. Obviously, not the right resident. The other two were mid to late twenties. Either was plausible. He grabbed a pencil, started to jot them on the notepad next to the computer, noticed the lower half of the top page was torn off. He remembered Kaylee had done so after she had written something down. He ran his fingers lightly over the exposed second page, felt indentations, shaded the same portion with the pencil. An address emerged. 1220 Latham Ave. #402. Obviously, not Kaylee's home address but where she was heading when she'd left the church. If she'd made it there, then it was her last known location before the bridge. Definitely worth checking out. He turned his attention back to the listings on the screen, jotted down the two probable addresses on the same piece of paper, ripped it off the pad, and shoved it in his pocket. He closed the internet tab, raised to leave. The door opened.

"What are you doing in here?" Pastor Williams stood in the doorway, a stack of papers in hand.

Drew stumbled for an explanation, finally said, "Kaylee's in danger. I'm trying to help."

"According to the news, you're the danger." Williams frame filled the doorway. He stood calm and straight.

"They got it wrong. I'm trying to help."

"So why don't you go to the police, explain it to them?"

"I can't do that....it's complicated."

Williams posture tensed, his eyes narrowed.

Drew said, "You have to trust me, Pastor. If I go to the police, Kaylee will die. I'm trying to stop that from happening."

Williams seemed unmoved, he said, "What happens if I call Arnold in here? He's retired military. I'm sure both of us could handle you while one of the ladies calls the police."

Drew looked Williams straight, said, "That won't be necessary. You're my brother in Christ. I would never fight you. I'm not trying to escape arrest. I'm trying to protect Kaylee. She's in trouble and I want to keep her alive. But, if this is God's will, then I won't resist."

The Pastor's gaze burned into Drew like he was reading his soul. Drew could see the Pastor was thinking, determining. Drew waited, didn't speak, kept his eyes locked with the Pastors hoping he could see he was telling the truth.

The Pastor's face softened, his posture relaxed, he said, "Look, I have to do what's right in the eyes of the law and in the eyes of the Lord. But, I do believe you. I came in here to use the copier. I'm going to do so. Then, I'm going to pray for you and Kaylee both. And then, I'm going to walk back to my office and call the police. I'd say that gives you about a ten minute head start."

He stepped aside. Drew thanked him and left the church.

CHAPTER FIFTEEN

Drew ducked into an alleyway behind a service station a few blocks from the church, crouched behind a dumpster, and pulled out the city map from his back pocket. He located the two street names from the White Pages search. Both were on the north side of town, one about five miles, the other several miles further still. The street Kaylee had written down, Latham Avenue, was four miles south west. Drew headed in that direction. Not just because it was the closest to where he was at, but because it made sense to follow her trail first, see where it led. If it ran into a dead end, then he'd try her residence. After all, her place was probably locked and he didn't like the idea of breaking in. But, under the circumstances, what other choice did he have.

The sun started to penetrate the dreariness

of the morning. The streets were drying up and Rocktown was waking from its Saturday morning slumber. Traffic increased. Drew stayed to the back roads, kept his hood up.

Latham Avenue was in a neighborhood of run down houses, low income apartments, and seedy looking filling stations. Most had bars on the windows and were marked with gang tags.

Drew found the address he was looking for at the end of the block; a four story complex built close to the street. It was old, brick, and checkered with a few stained air conditioning units. A woman stood out front. She wore tight cut off's and a blouse that left little to the imagination. Although, there wasn't much of her to imagine. She was all bone. Her cheeks were sunken, her eyes hollow. She looked as used as the neighborhood itself. Drew felt pity for the woman, wondered if she'd ever heard the gospel. If she had, she'd obviously rejected the message. Proverbs 13:15 came to mind- The way of the transgressor is hard. If ever there was a living testimony to this truth, this woman was it. Drew wished he had a tract to give her, knew as long as she was breathing there was still hope for her to be saved. He wished he could witness to her himself, knew he couldn't. Wouldn't be wise. These kinds of areas were heavily patrolled. He was surprised he hadn't spotted a cop already. A sliver of guilt pricked his heart. He told himself, that if God in His providence saw him through this, he would come back, tell her about Jesus then. But, not now. Now, he had to help Kaylee and find out who was trying to kill her. Ignoring the woman's suggestive grin, he made for the complex. The woman made a face, cursed him, and strutted off around the building.

The thumb latch to the entrance was missing. The door opened easy. A wave of hot air hit Drew in the face. It stank of alcohol and sweat. Bracing himself against the stench, he stepped inside into a small, shabby lobby. Just a simple squared room no bigger than a closet. The paint on the walls had peeled and the carpet was hard, grime colored. There was another door in front of him that he assumed opened into a hallway that led to the apartments. Next to the door, a narrow flight of blackened hardwood steps led upward, folded back and forth on itself several times all the way to the top. Drew took them, rounded his way to the fourth floor, and went through the door at the landing. Someone was blasting music with heavy bass and strong vulgarities. Drew hoped there weren't any children around.

The apartments were identified by tarnished brass numbers hanging on the doors. 402 was to his right. The door was open. He didn't see anyone inside, called out, heard nothing. He went in.

The apartment was an efficiency; no bedrooms, closet sized bathroom, and a pony wall sectioning off the kitchen. The whole thing was sparsely furnished, like something he would rent. There were no dishes in the sink, no groceries or appliances on the counter. Just some old Chinese takeout. Other than that, the place looked exceptionally clean. The stench of the building was less evasive. Cheap sheers tousled around at the window. A lace doily covered the coffee table. In the bathroom, a matching set of wash clothes and towels hung next to the sink and on the back of the door. On the arm of the tub, sitting in a small, circular rubber mat, was a half used bar of soap. It smelled of lilac. The medicine cabinet was empty.

Drew checked the closet next. A dozen or so hangers, several of which were on the floor. Also, crumpled up on the floor was a woman's blouse. Blue, short sleeved, plain in style. One distinct feature, the label on the collar read maternity. Drew dropped it where he found it, went to the kitchen, found some cleaning supplies in the cabinets under the sink. In the refrigerator was a used carton of milk and an opened can of peaches, the kind with the pull tab. Whoever put it away had left in a plastic spork. Drew closed the door, noticed a waste basket against the pony wall. Something was in it. He crossed the room, reached down and fished out an empty bottle of over the counter prenatal vitamins. Obviously, whoever was staying here was pregnant. A relative of Kaylee's? Someone she'd met at the clinic, maybe helping out? He didn't have much to go on, nothing with a name on it. No mail, no bills, no pictures. He wondered if the person still lived there. If they did, they were living with less essentials than he lived with, and that wasn't any way to live, not for a woman. Especially, one who was pregnant.

The music stopped. Voices bellowed from outside. Drew crossed the room, looked out the window. The bony woman was back. She stood directly below on the walk and was having a conversation with a cop parked across the street. Their tones were cordial, friendly. The cop called the woman by name, asked 'Heather' if she'd been keeping her nose clean. Drew stepped aside, figured it was time to leave before the conversation warmed up to "have you seen any strangers in the area?"

Drew didn't go the way he'd entered. He went to the other end of the hallway hoping to find another set of stairs that would lead to a rear entrance. Most apartment complexes of this nature had them. This one was no exception. As Drew neared the main floor landing, the door to the back lobby opened, and a massive figure walked in. It was Muscles, the gangbanger from the bridge.

For a second both men froze, locked eyes, recognition set in. Drew spun around, shot back up the stairs. Thunderous footsteps pursued. Good.

When Drew reached the top the music was blaring again. That was good, too.

He went through the door to the hallway,

rounded the corner, stood flat against the wall. Muscles came into view full throttle. Drew delivered a vicious backhand, felt bone splinter, and watched Muscles feet go out from under him. The big guy crashed to the floor hard. His breath left him in a single huff. Drew didn't retreat, didn't want to. What he wanted was answers. He straddled the man, leaned down and grabbed a fistful of Muscles Chicago Bulls jersey.

"What do you know about Kaylee Pierce?" Drew said.

Muscles looked dazed, but coherent enough. He muttered, "Who...?"

"The woman at the bridge!" Drew growled, "You know who I'm talking about."

Muscles eyes seemed to focus. Blood oozed from his smashed nose. His top lip was split and swollen. He smiles bloodied teeth, said, "Go to hell..."

"Sorry pal, got a Saviour who says otherwise."

Drew cocked back his fist intent on teaching Muscles the basics of how this little Q and A was going to go down. As he did, someone grabbed his arm from behind, yanked him back and spun him around.

A flash of steel!

Drew lunged to the side, avoided the thrust

from a knife aimed at his stomach and let the wall catch his fall. He whipped around. His attacker, the same guy who'd threatened to stick him at the bridge, was charging, knife in hand. Drew kicked him, caught him just below the sternum with his boot, sent the guy stumbling over his buddy and crashing into the door of an apartment. The guy was dazed. Drew shot forward, slapped the knife away, slid the man up the door by the front of his shirt, got real close, said, "You wanna tell me what's going on or you wanna play some more?"

The guy was scared, seemed to be considering real hard. And then, Drew was steamrolled into the thug; a hard, crushing blow, like being rammed by a freight train. The door gave and they spilled into the apartment.

Drew collapsed on the floor, tried to suck in air that wouldn't come and hugged his ribs. A blurred figure lay sprawled out next to him. Drew willed himself to move, rolled over and pushed himself up. Muscles staggered toward him, had something in his hands, above his head. A television set, tube style, square and heavy, and aimed right at Drew.

Drew swept his leg. It wasn't enough to take Muscles down but it did knock him off balance. He stumbled backwards. The television flew from his hands, shattered the widow and exploded on the pavement below. Heather yelled from outside.

Muscles charged. Drew was on his feet and ready. The conversation was over. It'd only take a minute for the cop to get up there, with back up on the way. Drew darted inside Muscles reach, an unsuspecting move telling from Muscles hesitation and look of surprise. Apparently, he wasn't used to people advancing on him. Probably was used to having people cower and shrink in fear at his size. He probably was used to fighting those smaller and weaker than himself. Easy targets. Or, maybe he was just used to fighting ten on one, like at the bridge. But now, it was one on one. Drew may have been smaller in height and weight, but he wasn't weak, and he wasn't an easy target. Muscles was about to find that out...the hard way.

Drew threw up an elbow, caught him under the chin, snapping his head. Using the same elbow, he delivered two more blows cross ways, forth and back. Then, he head butted him. It hurt, but not as much as it did Muscles. The big guy crumbled. Drew could have caught him with another blow on the way down but he didn't. Muscles was out cold.

Drew stumbled out of the apartment. The music had stopped again and he could hear heavy footsteps, and static from a police radio, fast approaching from the front entrance stairs. He wasted no time in heading to the other end of the hall, left the building out the back. A siren whaled and tires screeched from around front. Drew hurried down the alleyway, hopped a fence, and within a few minutes the scene was blocks away. He wasn't in any condition to track the other addresses. They'd have to wait. He needed to get his head together, regroup, rest. He headed for the train yard.

CHAPTER SIXTEEN

Drew opened his eyes. Moonlight seeped into the box car through the crack he'd left in the door, like he'd done the night before. Crickets chirped undisturbed outside. He must have dozed off, slept through the day. Just as well. The night cover would make the trek across town, to the north side, less risky, he hoped. He sat up slow. His muscles ached and his head felt heavy, like a cinder block. He dug through his duffle for a some aspirin he'd packed, took six, washed them down with one of the three bottled waters he'd also packed. The water was warm but it got the pills down. He finished the entire bottle in one swig and then sat back against the train car wall.

Kaylee had gone to see someone who was pregnant. Whoever it was must have been in some kind of distress. That's why Kaylee was concerned when she'd got off the phone, had to be. So, who was this pregnant woman and where was she now? Kaylee's? Made sense. If the person was in trouble, Kaylee could have picked her up, took her back to her place. It was a reasonable assessment. But what trouble? Muscles? He'd been at the bridge and at the apartment on Latham. He was involved somehow, that was certain. Maybe he was the one who'd hurt Kaylee, left those marks on her wrist. Maybe he'd caused her to go over the bridge, threw her off. But why? Domestic dispute? Had Kaylee gotten in the middle of a bad relationship between Muscles and someone he'd gotten pregnant? That was a probable scenario except for the camera. How did that fit in? It didn't. And, neither did the murder attempt at the hospital. No. There had to be more going on. But what?

Drew threw back his head letting it bang against the cold steel. He had Muscles right in front of him, could have made him talk. If he'd had more time. But he hadn't. And, so now, all he had was speculation and still no evidence of anything. Maybe he'd find something at Kaylee's. Maybe he'd find the pregnant woman. He got to his feet, threw up his hood and left the train car.

Within an hour, he cased the nearest address. The view through the large picture window revealed an African American couple. Not the residence he was interested in. He moved on to the next.

Another hour, he stood cloaked in the shadows across the road from a single story cape cod. The house was pitch. The curb stretched the entire block with no break which meant the drives were in back, accessible by alleyway. A single car was parked on the road a few houses down. From the shape, a Regal or some other type of Sedan. There was no one in or around it. Undercover? He didn't think so being there was no reason for the police to stake out Kaylee's house. As far as they believed, she wasn't in danger other than from himself and she was being guarded back at the hospital. At least, for the time being. There was no reason he could think of why they'd suspect he'd come here. But, even if they had, no cop worth his badge would have left his vehicle unattended in such an obvious location while on a stake out.

Drew darted across the road, climbed the steps onto the darker recesses of the canopy porch, knocked, not hard, just enough. No answer. He tried the knob. Locked. He peered through the window, through the crack in the blinds. To dark to make out anything. He went around the house.

The back door had a window, six separate panes covering the entire top half. The bottom right pane, the one near the knob was busted. Several shards of glass still hung in the fixture. There was none on the walk. The pane had been smashed from the outside. It looked like a break-in. The Regal came to mind. He tried the door. It opened. He stepped inside.

Drew was in the kitchen. He could just make the darker impressions of a sink, counter, a couple appliances, and a table. Everything was quiet. Nothing moved. He went to the counter, felt through the drawers until he found what he was wanted, a flashlight. Cupping the lighted end with his palm, he clicked it on. The glow was enough to let him get around without knocking into anything.

Someone's dinner was on the table. It looked days old, single setting. He left the kitchen through a wide archway, did a sweep of the place, noticed Kaylee's picture on the living room wall, knew he had the right address. She was posed with an older couple and had a strong resemblance to both. Her parents, probably.

Continuing to the other rooms, he readied himself for any confrontation. None came. Whoever had broken in was gone, if that was what had actually happened. The busted window could have just been an accident that Kaylee hadn't gotten around to fixing. Highly improbable, though. The house was well taken care of, clean and organized. She would have at least boarded it or something. And, it didn't make sense, a single woman living alone leaving such an easy opportunity for an evader to enter. He figured that's what she was, single and living alone, because the house was a one bedroom. And, there were no male articles of clothing, toiletries, or otherwise. Not that there would be. Kaylee seemed to be a devout

Christian. She wouldn't be shacking up with a man before marriage. Plus, other photos scattered around the living room gave no indication of a romantic engagement.

So, the back door probably was a break in. But why? What were they looking for? Maybe, it wasn't what, but who? A pregnant woman. Had they found her? Abducted her? There was no indication of a struggle. Everything seemed to be in place.

Drew retraced his efforts, did a more thorough search. Found nothing suspicious, or out of character, or anything that would suggest why someone wanted Kaylee dead. But there was something on the kitchen counter that did peak his curiosity. A newspaper. The Ebeneezer Tribune. From the header, he gathered it was independent, Christian, and conservative. The front page article was entitled- The truth about stem cell research. Next to the story, was a picture of the author. It was the same guy in the photo with Kaylee at her office. The caption under the picture read Herbert Freeman, freelance journalist.

A cord went around Drew's throat, yanked him back. He dropped the flashlight, tried to turn, punch, anything to pull free, but the cord dug deeper into his flesh. He couldn't breathe. His lungs burned, his ears rang. He brought up his foot, shoved against the counter, sent him and his attacker falling onto the kitchen table. It gave. They spilled onto the floor. The crash was loud. The attacker grunted. The cord loosened. Drew started to gasp but then the cord dug into his throat again. Pressure built in his head. His eyes felt like they were going to pop from their sockets. He rocked and flailed, knew he was dying. His hand slapped into something on the floor. A fork. He clawed at it, grasped it, and thrust it behind him, felt it sink into flesh. The attacker didn't scream, just grunted again.

Drew felt himself being pushed aside, the cord loosed from his neck. He gulped in air. Someone next to him was scrambling to rise. He willed himself to do the same. A hulking figure darted out the back door. Drew pursued.

Coming around the front, the Regal lit up, roared to life, and drove past. The passenger window was down. Drew could see the driver. His jaw was thick, his nose flat and crooked, like a boxer. Blood was streaming from his cheek. Pure hatred was in his eyes. He stared right at Drew as he went by, pointed a gun, and fired.

Dogs barked, windows lit up, and neighbors came out of their homes. It all sounded muffled, far away. Something sticky wet Drew's shirt. He realized he was lying face down on the ground. He'd been shot.

"Call the police!" someone yelled.

Drew got to his knees and then to his feet. His left shoulder burned like it was being seared by a branding iron and his arm dangled at his side. His legs buckled but he caught himself, half staggered, half crawled back around the house, to the alley. Sirens cut through the night air, closing in fast. He collapsed, heard tires skid in gravel a few feet away. A door opened. Everything was blurred and fading. A figure with strong hands pulled him to his feet, shoved him in a vehicle. Tires spun. Everything went black.

CHAPTER SEVENTEEN

Drew awoke to the sound of bacon frying. It popped and sizzled from the other room, smelled inviting. He lay in a bed, in what appeared to be a log cabin. Warm sunshine flooded the room through an open window. Outside were tall pines. Birds chirped.

Stripping back the covers, a flash of hot pain in his left shoulder reminded him he'd been shot. He eased his efforts, sat up slow. His shirt was off, his wound neatly bandaged. His arm rested across his chest in a sling. He touched his neck, where the cord had left its mark, felt salve. A short sleeved Polo, not his, lay folded at the end of bed next to his shoes. Taking his time, and careful to reinsert his arm back into the sling when finished, Drew dressed and exited the room.

The cabin was rustic, the furniture wood and crafted. A gun rack, cradling an antique double barrel rifle, hung on one of the walls of the main sitting area. Another wall held the head of a ten point buck. Across from the sitting room, to the right, Herb Freeman sat at a table pouring a cup of coffee, a plate of eggs and bacon in front of him. At his side, also with a plate of breakfast, was a girl. She looked to be about sixteen or so. And, she also looked to be at least six months pregnant. She didn't speak, just looked at Drew with doe eyes, somber and troubled.

Drew hesitated, unsure what to do.

Herb set the coffee pot on the table. "Relax, Mr. Richards, you're in good company." He motioned to another place setting, said, "Why don't you join us. I'm bettin' you could use a good cup of Joe."

As confused as Drew was, Herb was right. He could use a good cup of Joe. And, a plate of eggs and bacon wouldn't hurt either. He was hungry. He sat at the table. Herb made him a plate, handed him a steaming mug.

"You want anything in it, cream, sugar?"

Drew declined, stared at the old guy still feeling a bit apprehensive. He said, "It wasn't me, I mean, I didn't..."

Herb stopped him. "It's alright, Mr. Richards. I'm not sure how you're involved in all this, but I'm figuring you didn't do what the media's sayin'.

But, we'll get to all that in a minute. Let's say grace so breakfast doesn't get cold and Yvette here can feed that baby of hers."

The girl smiled, rested a hand on the crown of her stomach. Herb led in giving thanks to the Lord for their food, mentioned protection and healing for Kaylee.

They dug in.

Drew asked, "Who do I owe the honors of patching me up?"

Herb lifted his mug. "That'd be me. Medic assistant back in Nam. You got lucky, though. Bullet went straight through. All I did was clean and bandage. If I'd had to dig anything out, it wouldn't have been pretty." He washed down a mouthful, said, "I'm Herb Freeman, Kaylee's grand dad. This here's Yvette Taylor."

Yvette covered her mouth. "Hi."

"How far along?" Drew asked.

Yvette swallowed her food, smiled said, "Twenty nine weeks."

Drew took a sip of his coffee, said to herb, "I didn't hurt Kaylee. It wasn't me at the hospital. I mean, I was there, went to visit, walked in on a nurse, or who I thought was a nurse, injecting her with something bad. By the time I realized what was happening she was gone and I was left holding the bag, literally."

Herb nodded, not bothering to take a break from attacking his food. There was no suspicion in his eyes, nor his demeanor. He simply said through a mouthful of eggs, "So, that's it. Well, it's a good thing the Lord put you there when He did, Mr. Richards. Sounds like you saved Kaylee's life."

"Call me Drew. After all, you saved mine."

"Reckon I did, Drew." Herb wiped his mouth, said, "I went and checked on Kaylee earlier this morning."

"How is she?"

"No worse than before. There's an officer at her door. She's safe for now." Herb sat back. "Why don't you start from the beginning, though. Tell me what happened, everything you know."

"I know Kaylee's fall wasn't an accident. I know she wasn't in that area to enjoy the scenery. Had a camera with her. She must have seen or taken pictures of something someone wasn't too happy about. I know Kaylee's in trouble and I'm guessing, so is Yvette."

"Not bad. Kaylee was right about you. You are intelligent."

Drew shot a glance over his mug.

"Hey, what can I say, we talk. Spoke to her Saturday night. Let her know my flight wasn't coming in till late afternoon Sunday. She told me all about your meeting in the park. I will say this, you made quite an impression. And, she's got a good mind, good judge of character. That's why when Yvette and I saw you on the news, I knew they had it wrong. That, and knowing what else I know."

"Care to elaborate."

"Reckon I should." Herb paused to sip his mug, set it back on table. He said, "Kaylee was supposed to pick me up from the airport. Didn't show. And when she didn't answer her cell, I knew something was wrong. I caught a taxi over to her place. Her car wasn't in the drive so I let myself in. Found Yvette here, hiding in a closet, plum near scared to death. After I got her calmed down, told her who I was, she explained what was going on."

"So, what's going on?"

Herb and Yvette met eyes. Herb said, "It's alright. Go ahead and tell him everything you told me."

Yvette stared down at her plate, stirred her eggs, said, "I know Kaylee from the abortion clinic. I went there to..." she paused, didn't look up, said "I'm only fifteen, ran away from home last year. I was scared, didn't know what else to do. Kaylee talked with me, gave me some papers on God and stuff, said she'd help me and tried to get me to change my mind. At the time, I didn't believe her. Other people had said they wanted to help me, too, and they just..." her voice broke and she went silent.

Herb set a hand on her shoulder, "It's alright. Take your time."

Yvette looked up, made a weak attempt to smile, said, "I'm okay." She looked back at Drew, went on, "I was going to do it, have the abortion. But, the lady who worked there, the one who interviewed me, Samantha. She asked me all these questions, if I had any family, where I was staying, if I did drugs or alcohol, which I don't. I told her I hated the stuff. That's why I ran away in the first place. My mom would be so out of it she didn't care what her stinking boyfriends did..." Yvette shook her head, scoffed, "Anyway, Samantha told me about a client she had that would pay me a thousand dollars if I waited till I was twenty eight weeks before having the procedure..."

"Seven months?" Drew said.

"That's right." Herb spoke through a mouthful of food, "Seven months and illegal as all get up. At least for now."

Drew shook his head in disgust.

Yvette said, "Samantha said the fetal tissue, that's what she called it, said it'd be used for finding cures and stuff. She made me think I'd be doing something good. She got me a place to stay, paid for my food, came over once a week to see how I was doing and to give me checkups, like she was a nurse or something. I was fine with it for awhile, but then, the baby started growing. I could feel it moving and kicking. I started thinking about what it might look like, and if it was a boy or a girl. One day, I found the stuff Kaylee had given me. Must have gotten mixed in with my papers from the clinic. There was a booklet, the book of John. It talked about how Jesus is the son of God, and how He died on the cross for my sins and rose from the dead. It said if I believed in Him, God would forgive me of my sins, all the bad things I'd done, all my mistakes and the shame. He'd take it all away and God would accept me as His child. I wanted that. I wanted to be clean. I knew every word in that book was true. I asked Jesus to save me and He did. I know it."

Drew smiled, said, "That's great, Yvette. That's really amazing."

"It is. He is. I never would have thought...I mean, I didn't grow up religious or anything. I'd heard of Jesus, but I just thought He was like a fairy tale or something. But, He's not. He's real. I know that now. And, I knew I couldn't go through with the abortion. When Samantha came over, I told her what happened and that I wanted to keep my baby. She seemed happy that I'd found religion, said she had her own, too. I tried to tell her it wasn't religion but Jesus that saved me.

But, she was more concerned about the abortion. She told me I couldn't back out. That I had given written consent and was already being compensated. As far as her client was concerned my baby was their property and I was just a carrier. She said if I tried to run or went to the police, bad things would happen. She said a van would be there Sunday night to pick me up and take me to get it over with. She tried to convince me that when I had the money, I'd realize I did the right thing. I knew I wouldn't. So, Sunday morning, I called the number on the back of the booklet. Kaylee picked me up, took me to her house."

"Let me guess," Drew said, "Kaylee grabbed her camera, set out to get evidence to back your story."

"Yes. I told her not go, I really did..."Yvette's eyes started to well again.

"It's alright little missy," Herb said, "This isn't your fault. Kaylee's strong willed, stubborn as lock jaw."

"Funny, she described you the same way," Drew said.

Herb looked surprised.

Drew grinned, "Hey, what can I say, we talk." He set his empty mug on the table, said, "Sounds like this Samantha could be the one I saw at the hospital, the one who tried to kill Kaylee."

Herb made a face, hummed in agreement.

Drew said, "So, after Yvette filled you in, I take it you didn't go to the police for the same reason Kaylee didn't, no evidence. And, you couldn't report Kaylee missing for twenty four hours, right?"

"That's right. And, when they found her, they said her fall was an accident. I didn't want to risk bringing Yvette out of hiding until I could dig up something myself. Prove otherwise."

Drew scoffed, said, "I met the detective assigned to the case. I think you did right. Gotta admit though, all this over a single abortion. No disrespect, but how much can an aborted baby be worth, even at twenty eight weeks?"

Herb leaned forward. "That's just it. This thing's a lot bigger than one abortion. I did some digging." He looked at Yvette, "You might not want to hear this."

"I'll be alright."

Herb shot her a quick nod, "Okay then." He took a breath, said, "What I found was using aborted baby tissue for research is big business. We're talking a billion dollar industry. It's not so much the baby tissue, but the products produced by the research. Right now, you got labs injecting rats with aborted baby tissue to produce a cure for the common cold. Imagine how much that'd be worth if they succeeded. And that's just one example."

Drew said, "I take it the more developed the baby, the more viable for their experiments."

"Right."

"But what about the states that have legalized third trimester abortions? Some are even full term. Why not just get the tissue from there?"

"Many do. Even have legalized contracts with the abortion clinics. They send out technicians who are right there watching the procedure so they can bag up the body parts while they're still fresh."

Yvette's hand went to her mouth. Herb gave her an apologetic glance. He said, "But even those procedures are sanctioned to some extent. And you got to figure, this isn't a small market. There are organizations, investors, even our own governments involved. All with their fingers in the pie and racing to be the first to come up with these super cures. So, I reckon supply's in high demand. High enough to where someone's playing outside the sandbox. And I'm thinking it's not just some small fly by night shop. This whole thing is organized. It's someone with a lot to lose and their not taking any chances with loose ends."

"Makes sense," Drew said. "The guy at Kaylee's wasn't just some street thug. I'm betting someone pays him a lot of money to clean up loose ends. He wasn't there for me, though. Couldn't have known I'd show. Had to be looking for Yvette. What about you. Why were you there?"

Herb shrugged, "Not sure, really. I'd tracked Samantha that whole afternoon hoping she'd lead me to something but she just went to her place after the clinic."

"You know where she lives?"

"Sure do. Nice piece of real estate for just a medical receptionist. After hanging around there for most of the evening, thought I'd swing by Kaylee's. Didn't know what I expected to find, but sure glad I did."

"Me too," Drew said.

Yvette stood, started to gather dishes.

"You don't have to do that. I can get it," Herb said.

"It's okay, really. I need to do something to get my mind off all this. I'm scared. What are we going to do?"

Herb was quiet, seemed to be searching for an answer. Not the type to offer any false presumptions. Drew respected that.

Herb sighed, said, "I'm not sure, but God will see us through. We just have to believe that." He looked at Drew, "What about you, got anything?"

"Maybe. I saw the guy's plates, when he drove past, just before he shot me. California issued. Memorized the number."

"That's good. But how are we going to run them. It's not like the movies. No one at the DMV is going to oblige me that favor and I don't have an in with the police department."

Drew's gaze settled on the table realizing what was coming.

"What is it?" Herb asked.

Drew sighed, looked up at Herb, and said, "I do. Got a phone?"

CHAPTER EIGHTEEN

Drew stood on the porch of the cabin, in the shade of the overhang, and let his gaze survey the surrounding thicket of woodland. The only break was from a dirt road that wound to within a few feet from the porch, to where a crusted, Chevy Blazer was parked. Herbs cell was in his hand at his side.

Herb stepped out of the cabin, stood next to him, asked," So, how'd it go? You call your friend?"

Drew didn't break his gaze, just answered, "Rough. And yes."

"You alright?"

Drew smiled, didn't put much into it, said, "He's got a kid. Almost two. A boy. Named him Marcus Drew Sanchez." Drew shook his head, said, "I can't believe how much I've allowed pride and bitterness to take from me."

"At least you see that now. You know, you could have left town, went on the run. But you didn't."

"I couldn't leave Kaylee like that." Drew faced Herb, handed back his cell.

Herb grinned. His eyes were warm under thick gray brows. He said, "Don't reckon you could." He shoved his hands, with the cell, in the pockets of his jeans. "So, your friend run the plates?"

"They're registered to a company called Biogenetic Edge out of San Francisco."

Herb whistled.

Drew said, "You know them?"

"They came up in my research. Not one of the top feeders, but definitely an up and rising competitor."

"So, now we know who's behind this, what do we do about it?"

Herb scratched the scruff on his cheek, said, "I got a guy does research for me. I'll get him to see if Biogenetics have any connections out here. Get us some names."

Drew turned, stared back out at the woods, asked, "Where are we, exactly?"

"Bout fifteen minutes outside of town, why?"

"We already have a name. Samantha. Maybe we should pay her a visit. Tell her we know who she works for. Convince her the whole things coming down. Give her a chance to come clean, go to police with us."

"And if she doesn't?"

"Well, then we see what she does do. Like you said, this thing's organized. I say we rattle the cage and see where she runs for help."

Forty minutes after relaying the plan to Yvette and instructing her to keep the door locked, Herb drove the Blazer into a well to do subdivision on the east side of Rocktown. He parked in front of a two story, brick home with very elaborate and well maintained landscaping. Gesturing toward a silver Audi in the drive, he said, "She's home."

He and Drew exited the vehicle, followed decorative pavers to the front door. Herb rang the bell. The sun was high and hot, the landscape still. Herb rang again.

"Maybe she left with someone," Drew

offered.

"Maybe." Herb gave up on the bell, knocked.

A Persian cat emerged from beneath perfectly trimmed shrubbery. It coiled around Drew's leg, purred. Drew scooped it up, cradled it in his good arm. The cat didn't resist. Definitely well fed, at least fifteen pounds. Soft, gray fur hid the collar but the tags were visible. Tabitha. And an address. It matched the numbers above the door.

"Samantha's," Drew said.

"Is it declawed?"

"Yep."

Herb frowned, said, "Inside cat. So, how'd she get out?"

The men went to the side of the house, followed cement steps down to the back, to a large open patio and sliding glass doors. There were no blinds. Fresh scrape marks marred the frame at the latch and the door was slid open about a foot, just enough for the cat to have slipped out and just enough for someone to have slipped in. Drew caught Herbs glance, knew he was thinking the same thing. Drew set the cat down. Tabitha wasted no time springing toward the doors, darted inside. Drew and Herb approached a bit more cautious.

Through the glass, the kitchen looked spacious and clean. It ran into an even bigger and expensively decorated living room. The house was quiet, and dark. Drew called out, "Anyone home?"

Nothing. Herb shrugged.

They went in.

The main floor was undisturbed. Everything seemed to be in its place except for a half empty wine glass sitting on an end table next to the sofa. Upstairs, they found Samantha, dead. She was on her back, sprawled out on the carpet in the hallway. Her eyes were wide and lifeless, her lips pale. A thin red line ran around her neck. Behind her, the bedroom door was open. A jewelry box was spilled onto the floor next to a high end, designer vanity.

"Robbery?" Herb suggested. He didn't look at Drew, kept his gaze locked on the scene in front of him. His voice was steady, professional, but Drew noticed the old journalist's eye twitched and his jaw was set hard. Drew figured Herb was wrestling with the same indignation he, himself, was feeling.

Drew said, "Don't think so. I'm thinking it's staged."

Herb said, "Same here. Looks like she was

murdered by the same guy who attacked you?"

"Gotta be. Same M.O."

Herb asked, "How long?"

Drew nodded toward the body, at the purple discoloration showing on the underside of Samantha's arms and legs, said, "Couple hours, maybe longer." He frowned.

"What is it?"

"She's not the one who tried to kill Kaylee. I've never seen her before."

Herb's brows furrowed.

"I know," Drew said, "doesn't make sense...unless Biogenetics is doing more than taking care of loose ends. They're cutting ties altogether."

"Sure looks that way. But why? Because of Yvette?"

Drew shook his head, said, "I don't think so. She's just one girl off the street. It's hard to believe they'd consider her much of a threat."

"I don't reckon they would." Herb agreed, said, "But, maybe she's not the first, you know, to back out, to run."

"Maybe. But if so, no one's gone to the

police. Couldn't have, or it'd have been all over the media."

Herb rubbed his jaw, said, "If it got that far. Just like with Yvette, they'd need evidence. Without it, it's unlikely anyone would believe them."

Drew hummed his agreement. Herbs cell vibrated.

"It's my guy," He said, took the call.

Drew's attention went back to Samantha. A damp towel lay crumpled next to her. Snared in the tangles of her hair something glinted. A piece of necklace with an attached trinket.

Not wanting to contaminate evidence, Drew resisted the urge to pick it up, studied it from where he stood. A tiny, gold, five point star, in a circle. Looked religious. She'd told Kaylee she was. Drew suddenly felt pity for the woman, knew her religion would do her no good now. She'd gone to face her Maker without the righteousness of Christ, a child of wrath fitted for eternal destruction, according to the Bible. And, absolutely deserving of God's judgment. Everyone was, including himself. It was only because of God's sovereign grace that he'd embraced the gospel, receiving forgiveness of sins and in doing so, becoming a child of God. Samantha would never get that opportunity again.

Herb put away his cell, said, "We got something. Seems Biogenetics owns some warehouse property in our backyard. West Granite Lane. That's just a couple blocks from where Kaylee was found."

"You don't say."

"I do. And how much you want to bet it's filled with some pretty nasty medical equipment. "

"If they haven't cleaned house." Drew said, "I think it's time I give Detective Powers a call, bring him up to speed with what's happening."

Herb glanced at Samantha's corpse. "I think your right."

CHAPTER NINTEEN

"Who's up for roast beef and swiss?" Herb called from behind the door of the refrigerator.

Yvette fidgeted in a rocking chair under the buck head.

She said, "I'm sorry, I can't eat now."

Drew also declined, leaned against the frame of the picture window, and stared out at the silent dirt road, watched the shadows stretch out among of the darkened trees.

Herb dropped his fixings onto the table, said, "Think he'll show?"

"Said he would."

"Alone?"

"Gave his word."

Herb said, "Don't mean much nowadays."

Drew didn't answer, although he knew Herb was right. But, under the circumstances, what other choice did they have.

Yvette joined him at the window. She caressed her belly, looked up at him, said, "What if he doesn't believe me?"

"He will. And, with Samantha's murder, that'll warrant a full scale investigation."

"Not to mention media coverage," Herb said. He didn't bother looking up from his task. "This is big news. Going to draw a lot of attention. And when it does, you can bet there's going to be plenty of suits scurrying around like roaches."

Yvette stared out the window, said, "I can't help but feel bad for her. I wish she would she would have listened, you know, about Jesus."

Drew remembered Samantha's necklace, said, "Just curious, did Samantha mention what religion she practiced?"

Yvette chewed her lip, looked to be thinking hard, said, "Oh yeah, Wicca. That's what she called it."

Wicca. The term sounded familiar. But why?

He remembered...the book on Powers desk, the note, and the signature...Sam....*Samantha!*

Drew grabbed Yvette's arm, pulled her from the window.

"Hey!" Yvette yelped.

Drew looked at her. "We got to get out of here, now!"

Herb looked up, said, "What's wrong?"

"Powers, he's in on it!"

A gunshot echoed through the cabin. The kitchen window shattered. Herb reeled and fell to the floor.

Drew pulled Yvette low. Her eyes were wide and tearing. Her lips trembled. He motioned her to be silent. Herb didn't move. Blood pooled from underneath him. Drew pointed to the hall. They started to move.

The door to the cabin burst open. Yvette gasped. Drew spun around. A massive figure loomed over him. Muscles!

Drew tried to stand, caught a right hook, fell back into the rocker and toppled over. The punch fogged him. The pain from his wounded shoulder hitting the floor threatened to black him out completely. His arm was out of the sling, his shirt staining crimson. He struggled to get up, made it to one knee. And then, the cold, black, muzzle of Detective Powers Glock was in his face.

"That's right, Richard's, don't move. Don't even curl your lip or I'll blow it off."

Holding the gun firm, eyes locked on Drew, Powers dug out his cell, made a call.

No answer.

"Where is she?" Muscles said.

"How should I know!" Powers lost the cell in his pocket.

Drew guessed they were referring to Samantha which meant they didn't know she was dead. How could they unless someone had reported her missing or had found her body. And, apparently, that hadn't happened. Not yet, anyway. And, he hadn't told Powers anything when he'd called. He'd just set up their meeting, had planned on laying it all out when they were face to face.

Powers said, "Take the girl back to her apartment. Don't let her out of your sight. I'll be there as soon as I get things squared away here."

Muscles yanked Yvette to her feet by her hair, shoved her outside.

Powers glared at Drew. "All you had to do was get on the bus. I had the boys rough you up, so you'd get the message. I even told you myself, get on that bus. I didn't want this, Richards. You're a cop. And from what I read, a good one." The iciness in his eyes seemed to soften, although the gun in his hand didn't waiver. It still had Drew point blank right between the eyes. Powers said, "You know, you and I, were a lot alike."

Drew's lip throbbed. His shoulder burned and so did his anger. Powers was a bad cop. He'd broken his oath, had abused his position, and he'd hurt Kaylee.

"I'm nothing like you." Drew almost spat the words.

Powers scoffed, "Like I said, I read your file. You did your job. Saved that little girl and what do they do, huh! The ones you risked your life for every single day. They turned on you like animals. You and I, we have the same understanding. Give'em what they want, right. Let 'em destroy themselves. Only difference is, you let 'em take everything from you in the process. Not me. I got this deal going, Richards. All I gotta do is make sure no one starts poking their nose where it doesn't belong. Going to allow me to retire with a nice little nest egg. And nobody's taking it from me. "

"I forgive them."

"What?"

Drew said, "I forgive them."

Powers shook his head. His eyes narrowed, he steadied his aim, spoke through clenched teeth, "Well, I don't!" His finger tightened on the trigger.

Drew said, "Sam's dead."

Powers hesitated. His mouth opened but no words came.

"That's why she's not answering. We went to her place to give her a chance to come clean. Found her dead. Strangled. Seems Biogenetics doesn't forgive, either. Too many slip ups, to many girls getting away."

"I don't believe you."

"She's got a cat, right. Tabitha."

Powers face began to break at the edges. His eyes dropped a fraction.

Drew lunged.

Powers fired. Both men fell. The Glock skittered across hardwood. Drew shook off the ringing in his ears, got to his feet. Powers was scrambling for the gun. Drew went for the door, staggered outside. The world tipped. He fell off the porch, leaned against the blazer and stood. Powers emerged from the cabin.

He grinned venom, raised the gun.

Crack!

The detective dropped like a stone. Herb stood over him gripping the muzzle end of old rifle from the gun rack and had it lifted above his shoulder like a Louisville Slugger. Powers didn't move. If he was lucky, he was just unconscious. Drew couldn't say for sure. The swing had been solid. A homerun.

Herb lowered the rifle, went for Powers gun that lay next to the detective on the porch. He cringed and fell to one knee. Drew went to him.

"You alright?"

"It's not the first time I've been shot. I'll live." Herb dug in his pocket, retrieved his keys, held them out. "You gotta go after Yvette. I'll take care of Powers till the police get here."

"But..."

"Relax, I'm a reporter." Herb dug in his pocket again, held up a mini recorder, grinned, said, "Got every word. Now go!"

Drew started to turn, Herb stopped him, handed him Powers glock, said, "You might need this."

CHAPTER TWENTY

Drew parked a few houses down from Yvette's apartment building. The street was quiet, no one around. A rust colored cargo van was at the curb. Pieces of the television set still littered the sliver of yard and sidewalk. Through Yvette's busted out window, the light in her apartment was on.

With Powers gun in hand, Drew went to the rear of the building, used the back entrance.

The place was silent, no one in the stairwell, no voices, no music blaring when he slipped through the stairwell door onto the fourth floor. Something wasn't right. Set up? If so, he was ready.

Just like before, when he neared Yvette's apartment, the door was wide open. But this time, the apartment wasn't vacant. Muscles lay sprawled out on the living room floor in a pool of blood. Drew recognized him even before he stepped inside to investigate. Someone had put a bullet in his chest. Another gangbanger was in the kitchen, half lying, half propped up against the wall. He'd been shot in his forehead.

Drew checked the closet and the bathroom. Yvette wasn't there. He lowered his aim, leaned against the wall, fought the urge to collapse.

Biogenetics. Had to be. They'd snuffed out Muscles and his buddy fast and professional like. But why take Yvette? Why hadn't they killed her, finished the job. The police and media would chalk the homicides up as a gang war or something. Adding Yvette to the body count wouldn't have affected their conclusion. So why take her? Only one thing came to mind and it chilled him to his core. He pushed off the wall, hurried to the blazer.

Granite West Lane was lit by a single post. With some effort, Drew spotted the address above the door of a two story warehouse. It was dark, windows boarded. He cruised past the drive leading to the rear lot, parked at the curb of the next building. Keeping to the darkest shadows, he made quick to the front entrance. Debris and cobwebs told him the door hadn't been opened in years. He tried the knob anyway. Wouldn't budge.

Around back, he found the Regal with the California plates. The car was empty, parked next to a set of stairs that led to another entrance. The door was unlocked, opened with a click. The lights were on.

Drew made his way down the hall, checked each room. Besides some dusty office equipment and construction supplies, he found nothing. Rounding a corner, he came upon two sets of stairs, one leading to the upper floor, the other, to a sub level. He chose the latter, thinking it more plausible for an illegal abortion lab to be set up in the basement rather than an upper floor. The stairs ended at a long corridor, rooms on either side. Someone was speaking from inside one of them. A man. Drew could hear him clearly.

"It's the principle of the matter. Mr. Blackford made an investment. He wants his return. Simple as that."

Another voice groaned, soft, weak, sounded drugged. Yvette!

Gun raised, back against the wall, Drew made his way toward the groaning, stopped just outside the first room. The door was open. From inside, the man began to whistle. Items were being moved. Metal clanked on metal. Drew held Powers gun tight, steeled himself, and rushed in.

Yvette was strapped to an examination table. She wore a hospital gown and her legs were spread and secured to a set of stirrups. Her head shifted side to side, her eyes were open but lacked focus. At her feet, a man was setting a tray of neatly placed medical instruments onto a steel cart. He had on a disposable gown, like the kind hospitals give to visitors. On his hands, surgical gloves. One side of his face was covered with gauze.

"Hands up, now!"

The guy stopped whistling, turned slowly. Drew recognized the hate filled glare. He didn't flinch, kept the gun steady and pointed straight at the guy's chest.

"Nice and easy, step back...all the way to the wall."

The man did as he was told.

Drew stepped over to Yvette, transferred the gun in his slinged hand, undid one of the ties of the stirrups and then started on the arm strap.

"Drew..." Yvette's voice was feint, groggy.

"It's okay, It's ov...."

There was a flash of movement to Drew's right. He reeled. A scalpel came at him. He grabbed the wrist of its wielder, shifted the momentum of the thrust away from his face and rammed his good shoulder into his attacker. It was a woman, dark hair, the one from the hospital. Her petite frame was no match for his brawn. She flew across the room crashed into a counter and crumbled to the ground.

The man charged.

Drew spun too late. The gun was knocked from his hand. The man snatched him up by the shirt and flung him into the cement wall.

Drew hit hard, bounced off, felt large hands wrap around his neck, cutting off his air. He made an attempt to chop down the assault. No effect. The man's grip was like iron.

Face to face, saliva pooled at the corner of the guy's mouth. His eyes were glossed, animal like. He smiled, bared clenched teeth.

Drew felt his strength fade, sensed darkness overtaking him. On instinct, he sank a swift knee deep into the man's groin. His smile disappeared. His grip loosened.

Drew snatched the man by the back of head, yanked him in, smashed his face into cement behind him. Rounding on his attacker, he drove two consecutive punches into the man's gut. Both caused the guy to heave and he doubled over with the second.

"No!" Yvette yelled.

Drew looked back. The woman charged

again, scalpel raised.

Yvette's leg lashed out, kicked over the cart, spilling its contents in front of the woman. She stumbled, fell forward. Drew snatched up the guy, brought him around as a shield.

The man's eyes went wide. He grunted, uttered something, and then sank to the ground. The scalpel was buried in his back.

The woman gasped. She stepped back, her gaze wild and frantic. She turned, started for the door. Three officers rushed in, guns drawn, and halted her retreat. Herb was behind them. He ran to Yvette. Drew slid down the wall, watched the woman being handcuffed. A couple of paramedics entered. One headed towards him just as everything went black.

CHAPTER TWENTY ONE

"I want to thank you for saving my life." Kaylee said. She was sitting up in her hospital bed. The monitors, IV's, and bandages had all been removed and she'd been transferred off the ICU to a room on the lower floor for recovery and observation. Sitting at the edge of the bed next to her, Yvette chimed in, "Me too."

Drew placed a vase of flowers he'd picked up from the hospital gift shop on the window sill. He felt warm and it wasn't because of the sunshine streaming in. Both ladies were beaming big, syrupy smiles right at him.

He said, "It was nothing, really."

"Nothing!" Herb stood next to Drew, pointed at the Rocktown Star on the table tray, said,

"You made every headline in the country. Press is giving you full credit for taking down that whole operation. Biogenetics is done. You're a hero Drew, a real hero. And, I've already been given the go ahead to run a follow up story on what really happened with Manslow. People are going to know the truth."

There was a knock at the door. Kaylee's doctor entered.

"Just wanted to personally give you the good news. Tests have come back normal. There doesn't seem to be any long term damage. So, tomorrow morning you'll be transferred to a regular floor. I'd say within a couple days, you'll be clear to go home. You'll obviously have to go through some physical therapy, of course, but all in all, everything looks good."

Kaylee said, "Thank you, doctor. I really appreciate everyone taking such good care of me."

"Sure. I'm just glad everything worked out the way it did." The doctor turned to leave, stopped at the door, said, "You know, with the injuries you sustained, I can't explain how you're walking out of here in the condition you're in. You're one lucky lady."

Kaylee replied, "It's not luck, doctor. It's the loving hand of God. Can I give you something?" She grabbed a tract from off the table next to the newspaper.

The doctor cringed, said, "Whatever you want to believe. I'll pass on that, though. But thank you. Take care Mrs. Pierce." He left the room.

"Is there not a cause, right?" Drew said, offering a smile.

Kaylee nodded, smiled back, but there was sadness in her eyes. Beautiful sadness.

Herb said to Drew, "So, Yvette here tells me you're leaving Rocktown."

"You're leaving?" Kaylee said. She dropped her gaze, said in a soft, more reserved tone, "Where are you going?"

"Back home." Drew stepped to the side of the bed, looked down at Kaylee, said, "I want to thank you for inviting me to church. God did a work in my heart and I'm very grateful...to Him and you."

Kaylee didn't speak, just stared up at him with soft eyes.

Herb cleared his throat, asked, "When's your bus pull out?"

Digging his cell from his pocket, Drew checked the time, said, "Few hours from now." He noticed Kaylee's puzzled expression at the phone, said, "figured I might need one if I'm going to stay in touch with the people I care about."

Drew felt himself flush. Kaylee smiled and she started to color, too. She dropped her attention to her hands. Herb and Yvette were eyeing him, the corners of their mouths twitching. Drew quickly turned away, spotted the tract Kaylee had set on the table, said, "Do you mind if I take that? Someone I want to see before I leave."

Kaylee's expression sobered, although her face still glowed. She looked back at Drew, spoke reservedly, said, "Of course. So, you have a cause?"

Drew couldn't help but to grin, said, "I do Kaylee Pierce. I certainly do."

The End

Free Bonus Chapter

To get a free bonus chapter and to find out about other R.E.Antczak publications go to R.E.Antczak.com or visit R.E.Antczak on Facebook.

46318020R00074

Made in the USA
Lexington, KY
28 July 2019